Girl Fight

A UFC ROMANTIC COMEDY

BLAIR MONROY

Books by Blair Monroy

GIRL FIGHT SERIES

Girl Fight

Spring Blues

Summer Storm

Autumn Falling

Cover

Contents

Playlist

Copyright

Dedication

Books by Blair

PROLOGUE

Playlist

EVA'S

CUPID'S QUIVER | CUCO

VIGILANTE SHIT | TAYLOR SWIFT

WATCH | BILLIE EILISH

DEJA VU | OLIVIA RODRIGO

TAKE A BOW | RIHANNA

OBSESSED | MARIAH CAREY

SORRY NOT SORRY | DEMI LOVATO

ERIC'S

A GLIMPSE OF US | JOJI

GRANADE | BRUNO MARS

PICTURES OF YOU | THE CURE

DO I WANNA KNOW | ARCTIC MONKEYS

SLOW DANCING IN THE DARK | JOJI

LO QUE SIENTO | CUCO

Girl Fight

Copyright © 2023 Blair Monroy

All rights reserved.

This is a work of fiction. Names, characters, business, events and incidents are the products of the author's imagination. Any resemblance to actual persons, living or dead, or actual events is purely coincidental and not intended by the author.

Cover design by Aiden Kings

To my sisters, the best of friends.
Thank you for letting me talk your ear off about
my characters.
And thank you for being my best friends.

PROLOGUE

MY BEST CLAIM TO cynicism is that my best friend swiped my boyfriend. And my job, too. Okay, *fine*, not the job exactly, but she definitely pinched my boyfriend. In a totally painful, rip your heart out kind of way, too.

It all went down when I was a naive, wide-eyed twenty-four-year-old, convinced the world was my personal rom-com set. I had a best friend, a fool-proof three-step plan to take over the world, and a high school sweetheart. And life was good.

Spoiler: It all went tits-up.

Probably because of my colorblind optimism. While other girls sniffed out red flags like truffle pigs, I'd be like, "Red flags? I thought those were party streamers!" So when my boyfriend started "working late" and my bestie Tegan began "borrowing" my clothes (and, apparently, my man), I just clapped. *Go Team Us!*

The day it all imploded was textbook tragicomedy. I waltzed into work, high on pink clouds and ignorance, only to be summoned by my manager—a woman who styled herself as Miss Trunchbull's angrier cousin. She accused me of swiping a diamond bracelet, waving security footage of me delivering towels to Cabana 12 like it was the Zapruder film. "That's not theft," I argued. "That's customer service with a side of sabotage!"

But the pièce de résistance was later that day, when I spotted Tegan's Pantene-commercial hair flapping out of my boyfriend's truck, which was bouncing like it was auditioning for *Fast & Furious: Parking Lot Edition*. I stood there, a human PowerPoint slide titled How To Ruin Your Life In 10 Seconds, thinking, "Huh. Maybe those midnight 'gym sessions' weren't about squats."

I think back now and wonder if they'd been plotting for however long, saying things like, "Eva hasn't caught on yet?" "What a daft pig, that one. Let's make it more obvious, shall we?" "Oh darn, she's missed it again. I guess we'll have to do it *literally right in front of her* so she can finally get it through her thick skull that we've been laughing at her for the past however long. Then she'll get it. Har har har," and so on.

Tegan-fucking-Anderson—the perfect combination of Pamela Anderson (yes, even the last name, *ugh*) and Chucky (yes, the killer doll). And there she was, shaking that truck like a tambourine in a gospel choir.

It couldn't have been good, I'll say that much.

Four years later, here's what I know: 1) Cynicism is just optimism with a hangover. 2) Three-step plans should include "Beware of blondes." 3) True friends don't steal your boyfriend—they steal extra espresso shots for you.

So yeah, I traded a backstabbing BFF for one who'd mainline caffeine rather than men. And let me tell you, nothing pairs better with a croissant than *not* crying over spilled milk.

Progress, babe. Progress.

CHAPTER

ONE

❧

IT WAS SNOWING.

It sucked.

And I hated it here.

The Mojave had turned into the Swiss Alps in minutes. Snowflakes swirled like glittery betrayal while my car was doing a salsa routine on ice. I white-knuckled the wheel, muttering words that would make a sailor reconsider his career choices.

"Fucking snow," I grumbled, mad at the world. *And fucking people who like snow*, I thought, for good measure.

"Language, Eva!" Cali's voice chirped through the speaker, baby Rubi cooing in the background like a tiny, judgmental audience. "You're on speaker, and I'm trying to raise a decent human here." This from the older sister who once dared me to shotgun a Four Loko in a Taco Bell parking lot. Motherhood had turned her into a Hallmark card with goggly eyes.

"Sorry," I muttered, though I wasn't. The heater had chosen today to stage a *Hunger Games* rebellion, my scrubs reeked of regret and industrial-grade sanitizer, and I was freezing my ass off.

I punched the heater again.

"Strike one, bitch," I muttered, giving the dashboard a solid whack for good measure. Spoiler—it didn't work.

"Eva," Cali, dragged, and I winced.

I let out a long, dramatic sigh.

"You know stress ages you faster than UV rays, right? *Breathe.*"

"It's a healthy amount of road rage, Cal," I argued, gripping the steering wheel as my car did a perfect 10 ice pirouette. "God, I hate this snow."

"You know nothing's going to change whether you're mad or not, right?" her voice dripping with zen-mom energy. "Life is less about what happens and more about how you react to it."

I confirmed Christmas dinner and hung up before Cali could serenade me with another "namaste, babe" platitude.

Her toxic positivity was now rivaling the snow for Most Likely to Ruin My Day award. The café loomed ahead, a beacon of caffeine and sanity, and I had priorities: 1) Text Felicia. 2) Demand espresso. 3) Evict myself from this icy purgatory.

I thumbed out a message: "ETA 2 mins. Cortado scalding, raspberry tart warmed, my will to live crumbling. xoxo." And crawled my way through the (two) inches of snow. *Eye Roll.*

"An hour late," I announced to my windshield wipers, which juddered in solidarity. Finally free from traffic hell—*a ten-minute drive my ass, Maps*—I was ready to swap road rage for pastry therapy. My plan was a simple cortado so hot it'd melt my cynicism, a tart so buttery it'd grease my soul, and Felicia's gossip about the café's shenanigans to brighten my day.

It really was the perfect plan.

Until—

Bang. Bang. Bang!

Someone rapped on my window. I yelped, launching my keys into the void between seats. "For f—"

And there she was.

Tegan.

Four years older, four years prettier (translation: fillers and toner, probably), smirking through the glass like a *Gossip Girl* reboot villain. Her hair was sleeker than a Regency-era rake's sideburns, her coat cost more than my monthly rent, and her smile? Practiced. Polished. Poisonous.

My stomach plunged to my soggy Crocs. All my tough-girl bravado evaporated faster than a free sample at Costco. Suddenly, I was twenty-four again: heartbroken, clutching a lukewarm burger, watching her and my ex re-enact *Fast & Furious* in his truck.

No. No. No.

The universe wouldn't. *Couldn't.*

But there she stood, glinting in the snow like a rogue shopping cart—unwanted, unavoidable, and polished to a blinding shine.

Tegan-fucking-*Anderson*—AKA lowrider hydraulics.

I rolled down the window, arctic air slapping me awake. "Tegan?" I said, like I'd just spotted mold on my avocado toast.

"Oh. My. God!" She clapped, her bracelets clinking like a cash register. "Eva! *Darling!!* Has it really been *three years*?"

"Four," I said, my heart tap-dancing. *Jump out and throat-punch her*, I begged it silently. *I'll Venmo you.*

"Come here, you!" she sang, flinging my car door open. "Group hug! It's been way too long!" Her arms wiggled. I shivered.

There I was, dressed in scrubs that clung like Saran Wrap on a casserole, hair snow-splattered and dripping like a wet sock, and my *pièce de résistance*—socks with Crocs. This wasn't a reunion. This was a crime scene, and I was the disheveled exhibit A.

God, I hate her.

In the fanfiction version, this scene would've starred me in stilettos and a power suit, tossing a quip about karma over my shoulder. Instead, I shuffled out of the car like a sleep-deprived sloth, my Crocs suctioning to the slush. *Why hadn't I worn literally anything else?* Even flip-flops would've screamed "I'm thriving!" compared to this.

Tegan, meanwhile, looked like—well, Tegan. Legs for days, platinum hair so impossibly glossy it could've been used as a mirror by Renaissance painters, and a coat that whispered, "I have my own Instagram." Meanwhile, my coat was a thin athleisure number I'd bought because it had pockets.

I blamed Vegas. *Damn you, snow!*

We hugged. Or rather, I face-planted into her marshmallow jacket, inhaling a lungful of designer perfume and existential dread. She still towered over me like a six-foot snake.

(Translation: Crocs < heeled snow boots).

"Omygod, you still drive this thing?" She giggled, patting my lime-green junker like it was a rescued hedgehog. "So *vintage!*"

My eye twitched.

Strike two, bitch.

My car didn't deserve the slander. It chugged along faithfully, demanding nothing but gas station coffee and the occasional prayer.

I forced a smile, my fists clenching on their own volition. "Yep. Same car," I said, my tone flatter than a 2 a.m. pancake at IHOP.

And I'd probably still have the same boyfriend, too, I thought, *if you hadn't swiped him like a half-price Gucci belt.*

"You're adorable, Eva," Tegan cooed, her voice syrupy and sickly-sweet. "You never change!" Her eyes twinkled with the smugness of someone who'd just won *Squid Games* in designer loungewear.

"Guess what?" she plowed on. "I just upgraded!" She gestured to a Tesla so sleek it looked like it had been ironed. It crouched in the snow like a spaceship that had mistaken the parking lot for Area 51.

My nails dug into my palms. She'd always had a knack for weaponizing small talk.

"Anyway," she chirped, "why are you even out in this snow? Shouldn't you be... I dunno, cuddled up with your boo, watching *The Holiday* and sipping cocoa?"

I stared. In her defense, it had been four years, and it wasn't her fault I'd been on a self-imposed man-ban since she'd swiped my last one.

Her eyes widened. "Oh, *right*! Well, at least you've got a real job now!" She eyed my scrubs—clinging like cellophane on a wet dog—with a look that hovered somewhere between pity and disdain.

"Real as it gets," I said, my tone dry. *Yes, Tegan. Some of us actually work for a living. Not all of us can float through life on a cloud of privilege and perfectly toned hair.*

Sure, my love life was a *Bridget Jones* diary entry, my car doubled as a rolling freezer, and my weekends revolved around Felicia's caffeine IV drips and café drama. But at least I had dignity.

The only thing between me and a Netflix doc titled *Woman Throws Croc at Tesla: A Cautionary Tale.*

Tegan's smile flickered like a filter glitch—there and

gone—before she plastered it back on, brighter and shinier than a fresh coat of lip gloss. "Don't tell me you're here to stalk the gym hotties?" she trilled, laughing like she'd just invented comedy. "Kidding!"

"Just grabbing a friend," I said, jabbing a thumb at the café like an unsuspecting idiot. *Why did I say that?* I knew better. Bad friends were a thing of the past, but the past was staring right at me and my sopping wet hair.

"Twins!" Tegan chirped, and I knew she had a bomb waiting for me. "I'm here to see my boyfriend."

Boyfriend.

The word oozed out of her mouth in slow motion.

"He just joined this gym," she added, pointing to the MMA studio I'd walked past approximately 9,000 times and never noticed. "He's a UFC fighter. Super famous."

If I didn't know her any better, I might've assumed she was just sharing the news. But, of course, I did know her. I don't know how, but I knew she knew. She knew I was single. She took one look at my Crocs and said, "Eva's still single! I win!" And now, her chirpy one-upmanship lit a fuse in me—a fuse attached to a very petty grenade.

"Oh, I've seen him!" I said, channeling the lie from deep within me. "He's sweet. Never mentioned a girlfriend, though."

Tegan's smile froze mid-air like a screensaver, and I felt a flicker of triumph. My grin widened—the first genuine one since this reunion began, and probably the last until my next cortado.

Her eyes narrowed into lethal slits, but her lips stayed curled in a Botox-defying smirk. "Oh, he definitely has a girlfriend. *Me*," she purred. "Some men cheat and lie, Eva, but others don't."

The jab hit like a prickling up my neck. "Funny," I shot back, "you would know all about that, wouldn't you?"

Clang. The gym door swung open, and Tegan jumped like she'd been caught smuggling contraband Spanx. "So lovely catching up!" she trilled, already backing away. "Let's do this again soon!"

Let's not, I thought. "Can't wait!" I chirped, matching her tone like a passive-aggressive parrot.

She air-kissed my cheek—her perfume smelled like Regret by Chanel—and flounced toward the gym. Just then, he emerged: Tall. Brooding. Abs that could grate cheese. The kind of man who'd make taking out the trash look like a Calvin Klein ad.

So this was Mr. Super Famous UFC Fighter? From afar, he

was… fine. If you're into chiseled jaws, biceps like cantaloupes, and the aura of a man who'd never lost a game of Scrabble.

Before I could spiral, Felicia exploded out of the café like a cortado-powered tornado. She thrust a to-go cup at me, steam curling like a tiny white flag of surrender.

"Get in here!" she hissed, waving me to the café's warm sanctuary. "It's freezing out here!"

"Just… let's go home," I mumbled, suddenly aware my Crocs were now half ice, half regret.

Felicia vanished, reappearing with a tart clutched like a grenade. I stood frozen, watching Tegan giggle at UFC Hunk's jokes. Snowflakes melted into my hair, my scrubs, my soul.

"Bitch," Felicia barked. "You just got the best cortado of your life—Oh my god!" She elbowed me, nodding at UFC Hunk. "That's the little snack I keep texting you about. And, I mean, there's nothing little about him, if you know what I mean."

I sipped the cortado. It was, admittedly, divine. "He's… something, alright."

"Something? Eva, he's not just a snack. He's a three-course meal! A—"

"Shh!"

I practically dive-bombed into my car, shooting Felicia a look that screamed "Shut it!" in neon lights. Didn't want Tegan overhearing us, especially since she was approximately 2.7 feet away. Felicia vaulted into the passenger seat, vibrating like a Chihuahua on a Red Bull bender.

As I yanked the seatbelt across my chest, I stole one last glance—praying UFC Hunk would morph into a goblin as he inched closer. No such luck. He was still stupidly hot, even wrapped in layers like a burrito.

"Is he hot?" I lied. "Hard to tell under all those clothes."

Felicia snorted. "Are you dense? I turn red every time he comes in for coffee."

I shrugged.

"Oh—look! He's with a girl. And a pretty one, too." She sighed dramatically. "Is that why you gave me that look? I should've known—everyone wants the little snacks. I bet he's got a big—Oh my god, do you see that? Eva, that's not a dick print, that's a dick billboard!"

I risked a peek in the rearview. Tegan was sliding into her Tesla, waving like we'd just bonded over mani-pedis instead of emotional warfare. Against my better judgment, I waved back while my soul cringed.

"Let's go home," I muttered, revving the engine. My lime-green junker roared to life and backed out excruciatingly slow. *Thanks, snow!*

"Spill," Felicia demanded, licking tart crumbs off her thumb. "What's the tea with that girl?"

I white-knuckled the wheel. "Long story short, she's the reason I spent three years in therapy."

Felicia's eyes went wide. "Fucking hell. She's that bad?"

"Worse," I retorted, stealing one last glance in the rearview mirror. Tegan's Tesla was already off, but her smug smile was still seared into my mind.

Felicia patted my arm. "Cheer up, babe! At least we've got tarts, caffeine, and each other."

"Yeah. At least we have that."

CHAPTER
TWO

YESTERDAY'S SNOW HAD VANISHED faster than a free luxury perfume sample, leaving behind a sky so blue it looked Photoshopped. I floated through the morning, buoyant as a helium balloon, my grumpy snow-day alter ego firmly in the rearview. Or so I thought—until Tegan buzzed into my brain like a wasp at a picnic.

Running into her yesterday had been less "chance encounter" and more "stepping on a Lego barefoot at 3 a.m." And now, thanks to her UFC boyfriend—a man whose sweatpants should come with a parental advisory sticker—she was basically my neighbor. His new gym was two doors down from the café. Because the universe apparently thought, "You know what Eva needs? A daily reminder that her love life is a barren wasteland!"

Let's just say his gym attire was *educational*. Four years of self-imposed celibacy? Gone. Obliterated. Reduced to ash by a man who looked like he'd been carved by a Renaissance sculptor with a very specific commission. Every time I glimpsed him, the universe cackled, "Remember Tegan's winning streak? Here's Exhibit A!"

And that's exactly what his sweats said next I saw him, on a routine Felicia pick-up. I wasn't planning on running into anyone, especially not in my Crocs again (no, I hadn't learned). And no one could say I was on the pull in my unbrushed hair pulled into a messy bun.

I'd have worn a sleek one, of course.

I'd been innocently lurking in my car, plotting evasion tactics worthy of Jason Bourne, vowing to become invisible for as long as it took. Tegan'd be my neighbor for however long she kept that boyfriend (which, in Tegan's world, likely wouldn't be long anyway). I'd drive in, grab Felicia, peel out like Dom Toretto with a caffeine addiction. Simple.

But then he emerged from the gym, sweatpants clinging like they'd been painted on, and my brain short-circuited. There he was, leaning against the gym wall like a misplaced Abercrombie model, covered in sweat, dressed in the same sweats from yesterday, I think. Only I wasn't really looking— today or yesterday.

Before my brain could scream "Abort!" my traitorous hand honked the horn. *Why?* Maybe the Four Loko of courage I'd chugged in 2016 finally kicked in. He turned, squinting against the sun, and I waved like we were co-stars in *How to Lose a Guy in 10* Minutes. A thrill ran through me, something sharp and wicked. A naughty little thought that said maybe I was on the pull, after all, and what of it.

I swung my car door open and stepped out, each step felt like I was floating—or maybe hallucinating. My heart pounded like a washing machine on spin cycle, and no, it wasn't the cortado.

The gym behind him looked like a Soviet-era bunker someone forgot to decorate. No flashy sign, no neon arrows —just a tiny plaque by the door that read Iron Forge in block letters. I bit back a nervous laugh—he was a professional fighter, after all. Probably punched people for less.

He was bent over, heaving like he'd just outrun a bear. I took my first good up-close look. It was the aglets that caught my attention. They weren't the same sweats. You see, yesterday's drawstrings had silver aglets. Today's were black.

"Hi," I blurted. My heart almost leaped out of my chest because, well, it was at that very moment that I thought, *this is Tegan's boyfriend, you hag.* "I've never seen you around here," and I said it casually enough that even I believed it.

He straightened, wiping his brow. His eyes flickered to mine with a sweet smile that seemed to say, *You're talking to me?* He looked surprised, and I could see the slight squint in his eyes as if processing that I was the one initiating a conversation with him. As if he too was thinking, *Tegan won't like this.* His mouth twitched. "That's funny," he said, voice low and sandpaper-rough, like he hadn't used it in hours. "Because I've seen you."

If I hadn't been mid-crisis over my first proper full-face look—all jawline and full lips—I might've collapsed. Or clung to the wall like a starfish, because shouldn't he have said something like, *Sorry? I don't talk to people my girlfriend hates, especially not ones in messy buns and ugly Crocs.*

But god, was it a good full-face.

My first thought was, *yeah, this is the kind of man Tegan would pull, wouldn't she.* On second thought, maybe it wasn't. Some lanky post-teen with a penchant for club bouncing, maybe (bye, stupid ex). But this guy? He was all kinds of right.

"You're kind of hard to miss in that lime-green car."

I laughed—a sound halfway between a cackle and a seagull choking. "It's not the car," I said, words tumbling out like loose Skittles. "It's the girl."

Oh god. Did I just… flirt? With Tegan's man?!

"What can I say?" He shrugged, sweatpants doing things

I refused to acknowledge. "It's always the girl."

Well.

Was it Fourth of July? Because the fireworks were going off.

My bravery screeched to a stop. "I should go. Maybe my lime-green ass can hold your attention this time." And there it was. Again.

"Is that an invite?" He straightened, towering over me like a redwood tree.

His eyes—big, blue, and darker than the ocean—locked onto mine. A spark fizzed between us. Or maybe it was just static from my socks?

I wasn't planning on backing down, either. But then something caught my eye. Something white, sleek, and familiar.

A Tesla.

Her Tesla.

Tegan's voice sliced through the air, killing the moment. "Hey!" She stormed toward us, heels clacking with a fury against the pavement. Her eyes narrowed to slits. "What's going on here?"

When Dick Print (too on the nose?) didn't immediately

respond, I felt the pressure on me. And it wasn't like I'd made any covenants to her like I imagined Dick Print had—*will you be my girlfriend? I promise to be loyal and* faithful—but he just had a sly smile on his lips.

Dick, indeed, then.

I braced myself, ready to fight. "In fact—"

But my little moment of bravery was abruptly interrupted when Guy Arter, the café owner, materialized beside me like a cryptid from a caffeine-fueled nightmare. I nearly vaulted into the stratosphere as his leathery hand landed on my shoulder.

"You'll fry like an egg out here, kid," he croaked, steering me toward the café with the subtlety of a bulldozer. His face, weathered like a cowboy's saddle, crinkled into a sage-like nod. "Take it from me—sun's a cruel mistress. Walk away before you blister."

I blinked. "Is this a metaphor?"

He ignored me, squinting back at Tegan and Dick Print. "Go wait in your radioactive green car. I'll fetch Felicia."

"You heard all that?"

"At my age, I hear my joints creakin' and my regrets louder, but body language screams. Now *shoo.*"

"What the *hell* was that?" Tegan's voice sliced through

the parking lot. My brain screamed "Don't look!"—but my neck, ever the traitor, swiveled like a revolving door.

I had a little tiny moment of satisfaction when Dick Print said, "Oh, come on, Tegan. I don't have time for this," but then they walked in the gym and the door closed behind them and it was all over before it had even begun.

Felicia was going to have a bitch when I told her.

A smirk crept onto my lips. Who knew petty defiance felt this good? It was like eating a whole tub of ice cream *and* skipping Pilates.

It wasn't long before Felicia cannonballed into the passenger seat, eyes sparkling like she'd mainlined espresso. "*Bitch*. Were you just WWE-smackdown-ing Tegan?"

"What? No! Is Guy gossiping again?" I groaned. Café people were worse than TMZ. "It was nothing like that."

"Well, Guy said something about a tall blonde getting ready to beat the crap out of you. And let me guess..." She put her finger on her chin, pretending to think. "The only blonde I know is Tegan."

I slumped, cheeks burning like I'd face-planted into a jalapeño. "Okay, fine. I maybe sorta poked the bear. With a tiny stick."

Felicia gasped, pushed a curl behind her ear. "Eva! What

if she'd karate-chopped you? Or worse!"

I flopped back, finger-combing my messy bun. "Relax. I just said hi. It's not like I gave him a handsy or anything."

Felicia nodded slowly, but her smile wasn't one of approval—it was that look she gave me when I'd done something risky. Something reckless. "Glad it was worth it," she said, voice dripping with judgment. "But if Tegan had gone full *Tiger King* on you, I'd have had to choose between filming it or tackling her. Next time, at least wait for me."

I gnawed my lip, imagination running wild. Hair pulling, name calling, cat scratches. *Oh, god*. "Yeah, you're right. I was being stupid. Never again."

"Never again," Felicia echoed.

Felicia wasn't exactly the patron saint of good decisions herself. Quitting law school had been mild. Getting disowned by her parents after exposing her dad's "creative accounting" (i.e.: felonies)? Now, that had been TMZ worthy drama. Now she clung to Guy like he was Gandalf and she was Frodo, despite him mostly offering flour, butter and 80 hour workweek.

She tucked a curl behind her ear, voice softening with the unmistakable sound of curiosity. "But how was he?"

"Dick Print?" I fanned myself like a Victorian heroine.

"Oh, god. His voice. Like if an ASMR narrator and a gravel driveway had a baby."

She giggled like a school girl. "Right? Deep, just the right amount of rasp. Mmm."

"He said he's seen me before."

"Seen you?!" Felicia gasped. "Pack your bags. You're eloping. I'll officiate."

We zipped home, talking and laughing like a couple of virgins about to have their first kiss. It wasn't so far fetched, either. While I hadn't dated anyone since my slimy ex, Felicia didn't shy away from the annual one-nighter, though the year was fast creeping on. Maybe Felicia didn't keep a calendar of her escapades, but I sure did. And baby, we were *starving*.

Back at our apartment—a cozy shoebox we'd decorated with thrifted art and questionable life choices—Felicia popped rosé and I flopped onto the couch, still buzzing.

"Wait," I said, wine sloshing dangerously. "What's his name, anyway?"

Felicia did that little side tilt with her head. "I actually don't know."

I sipped my rosé, a mischievous grin spreading. "So ask him next time he orders. Bat your lashes, drop a pen, 'Oops, need your name for the cup!'"

"Guy banned us from Starbucks-style ordering," she said, brow furrowing. "He thinks it's 'undignified.'"

"Booooo," I groaned, though my brain was already drafting scenarios: Me, "accidentally" spilling cortado on Dick Print's shirt. Him, laughing, peeling it off to reveal— *Focus, Eva.*

"But..." Felicia's tone shifted, her eyes widening like she'd just remembered we'd left the oven on. "There's something else. About Tegan."

My stomach did a Cirque du Soleil routine. Not just because Tegan had nearly turned me into a parking lot pancake earlier, but because her name alone was cursed— like Bloody Mary. She had a knack for haunting my life like a pop-up ad you couldn't close.

Gossip was always more fun when it was about someone else, wasn't it. Someone distant, someone unconnected to your own life. But Tegan? She was the human equivalent of a browser history I'd tried (and failed) to delete. And now, with Dick Print orbiting her like a moth to a flamethrower, she'd upgraded to trending topic.

I schooled my face into "I'm fine!" mode, but the rosé betrayed me. "What about her?" I asked, voice careful.

Felicia hesitated, twisting a curl around her finger like it held state secrets.

"All's not well in *casa* Teflon Tegan."

Well, well, well.

CHAPTER

THREE

"EVA, PREPARE YOURSELF," FELICIA announced, her voice buzzing with excitement. She fanned herself with a napkin, despite the fact it was colder than a penguin's picnic outside, and leaned in like she was about to disclose nuclear codes. "Tegan finally got what's coming to her."

I gripped my wine glass so hard the glass whined. "Felicia, I swear to god, if you don't spit it out—"

"I saw them!" she hissed, eyes wide enough to reflect my caffeine-deprived despair. "Dick Print and Teflon Tegan! Together! In the wild! And let me tell you—" She paused, savoring the moment like a soap opera villain mid-monologue. "—their 'perfect' romance? Less stable than her lash extensions."

"Ohmygod, they're fighting?"

"Well, not exactly, but guess what? He looked pissed.

Like, 'I-just-found-out-she-stole-my-identity' pissed. Steam was practically shooting out of his ears! He's basically a human teakettle in a Tom Ford suit." She leaned back, smug. "Your ex-nemesis is vulnerable to attack. This is your moment."

I blinked, thoughts jumbled. "My moment for what, exactly? Sending a fruit basket labeled 'Karma's a Bitch'?"

"No! Your moment to swoop in." Felicia mimed a dramatic hair toss. "Steal her man, steal her life, steal her weirdly specific latte order—whatever. The point is, she's vulnerable! And he's hotter than that time Shane accidentally set the espresso machine on fire."

"Felicia, this is unhinged," I said, though a tiny, petty part of my brain was already drafting a PowerPoint titled Operation: Dick Print Revenge.

Felicia sipped her drink, eyes gleaming over the rim. "Just picture it: you, gliding into her brunch, arm-in-arm with her man, wearing her favorite designer. She'd spontaneously combust. *Poof!* Nothing but ash and regret. Well deserved, mind."

"You literally just gave a TED Talk on 'Eva, Don't Stab Tegan With a Spork!'" I shot back, half-laughing, half-wondering if my inner petty gremlin was taking notes.

Spoiler: It was. But I'd sooner wear Crocs to a gala than

sink to Tegan's level. *Probably*.

"I said 'don't confront her alone,'" Felicia clarified, waving a hand. "Not 'let her keep Dick Print'! That man's a renewable resource, Eva. Reclaim him! Recycle him! Compost her wet dreams!"

"Or maybe," I countered, "they were just arguing about whose turn it was to buy lattes. Ever think of that, Sherlock?"

Felicia rolled her eyes so hard I heard her retinas snap. "Please. My gossip radar is *never* wrong. It's like Spidey-sense, but for drama. And right now, it's blaring: 'Tegan's empire is crumbling! Send in Eva!'"

My brain buzzed with possibilities—name calling possibilities, that is—each more judgmental than the last. Home wrecker. Adulterer. Seductress. Temptress? Okay, maybe not temptress—that felt a bit too glamorous for the situation. Tease, though? Definitely tease.

"I don't do taken men," I said firmly, inspecting my nails like they held the secrets of the universe. "Or Tegan's sloppy seconds. Karma's got this. It's just slow. Like a sloth on melatonin."

"Karma's asleep," Felicia snapped. "Wake it up! Throw a parade! Hire a marching band!"

I couldn't help but feel a tiny flicker of smugness when I

thought about Tegan's reaction outside the gym. Showed she at least had the possibility to feel jealousy—caused by yours truly. Honestly, I'd surprised myself by even going there. Schadenfreude was my new favorite Netflix genre.

"Fine," I groaned, surrendering to the gossip gods. "Tell me everything."

Felicia leaned in, eyes sparking like a pyromaniac at a fireworks factory. "Okay, so." Her voice dropped to a whisper. "Dick Print waltzed in today, looking like he'd just stepped off a Calvin Klein billboard. And then—" She paused, savoring the moment. "—he asked for the usual order. Cappuccino, extra foam, extra cocoa." Another pause, this time to sip wine like she was in a slow-motion ad for "Gossip: The Beverage." Then she leaned in, her flair for the dramatic showing.

"But this time," she said, "I kept it together. Barely. I think it's because he's officially off the market now. And for some reason, that made him less intimidating? Like, I always knew I didn't have a shot, but now that he's taken, it's like he's, I don't know, safer? Does that even make sense?"

I nodded because, honestly, unattainable men are the best kind of eye candy. No awkward small talk, no accidental hand brushes over a cappuccino, just pure, guilt-free ogling. It's like window-shopping at the Aria—you can admire, but you're not dumb enough to max out your credit card.

"Anyway," Felicia said, her voice low and delicate, "Tegan strutted in after him, same as always. But today? Oh, honey, I bet she wishes she'd stayed in bed. The tension was thicker than the smoke in one of those old casino carpets—you know, the ones that smell like regret and cigarette stench. And then—*bam!*—he recoiled like she was a hot coal. Subtle, but I clocked it. And Tegan just smiled away like nothing while he inched toward the exit like it was an all-you-can-drink margarita bar. And then—" She paused, leaning in. "—he eye-rolled. Not some polite, 'Oh, Tegan, you're so quirky' eye-roll. No, this was a full-on, 'I'd rather be in Pahrump eye-roll. You couldn't have missed it if you were on the dark side of the moon."

She took a theatrical sip of her rosé, letting the gossip simmer like a fine stew.

I barked a laugh. "Swear."

"Swear!" Felicia crowed, her grin sharper than the time we spotted her ex at a bus stop. "It was like watching a seagull steal a fry—brutal, brilliant, couldn't look away."

Tegan's golden boy, eye-rolling like she'd suggested a weekend in Pahrump? It was the petty vindication I didn't know I needed—like finding out your ex's dumb truck got towed. Not that I'd lift a finger, mind. Karma's got better things to do, like fixing the Spaghetti Bowl and maybe the Strip during Super Bowl. But damn, it tasted sweeter than the Christmas tres leches cake at Cali's.

Tegan's life was a dupe Vogue spread—all blowouts and brunch pics, zero mention of the 3 a.m. meltdowns over FashionNova returns that didn't fit. Her superpower was turning dumpster fires into "aesthetic chaos" with a Valencia filter and a #Blessed caption.

"She conveniently skipped that chapter," I snorted. Ugly, but effective.

Tegan's MO was simple: stab you in the back, then post a selfie with a caption like #WomenSupportingWomen and a heart emoji. Her Instagram was a highlight reel—all rooftop cocktails, none of the hangover. But those little cracks in her veneer were my guilty pleasure.

Felicia's smirk widened like she'd just won the lottery. "Think she'll waltz in later and shove her 'perfect' relationship in our faces? Perfect life, my ass."

But the seed was planted. Pedestals are precarious things —all it takes is one little push. And if that push came from me? Well, let's just say I'd channel my inner Lisa Rinna and *own it*.

Not the healthiest coping mechanism, sure, but cheaper

than therapy and twice as satisfying.

"He hates her. I'm telling you," Felicia declared, with the confidence of someone who'd binged every season of *Love Island* twice. "Bet he's only with her because she looks like an overpriced call girl at the Ritz who's one champagne flute away from getting kicked out."

I snorted, nearly spitting out my wine. "Oh, he's definitely with her for the looks—god knows her personality's flatter than an Olipop left out all night." The words tumbled out before I could stop them. My therapist would've scribbled "regression!" in her notes, but Felicia's cackle made it worth it.

"But I don't know, Fel," I added, trying to sound mature and failing spectacularly. "Every couple has their moments. Maybe they just argued over who forgot to buy the milk."

Felicia arched a brow, unimpressed. "Look at you, playing devil's advocate."

"I'm not."

"And I'm serious. My Spidey senses were tingling."

I slumped back in my seat, staring at my cracked iPhone screen like it held the secrets of the universe. "Guess her Instagram filter's finally cracking, then."

Felicia nodded, her grin sharper than a sushi knife.

"'Bout time. Can't polish a turd forever, can you?"

I didn't say it aloud, but the petty gremlin in my brain was hosting a full-blown rave. Tegan had always glided through life like she'd been born with a diamond-encrusted spoon and a personal entourage of luck, leaving the rest of us clutching Trader Joe's reusable bags in a downpour. But now? The cracks in her facade were widening like a cheap pair of leggings, and it was glorious.

Was I about to sabotage her curated existence? Please. I wasn't a monster. But I'd be lying if I said I wasn't itching to grab popcorn and watch karma finally clock in for overtime—karma, bless its cotton socks, now armed with a Red Bull and a to-do list.

Suddenly, I felt lighter, like I'd traded my emotional baggage for a Marc Jacobs tote. The sun dipped low, smearing the sky in hues of blue and purple native to Vegas. I flung open the kitchen window, letting the crisp air rush in. It smelled like victory and possibility—or maybe that was just Felicia's aprons fermenting in the laundry room. Either way, it felt like a fresh start.

Let's be honest. Was I devastated that Tegan's life wasn't the fairy tale she'd Instagrammed? No. Was I ugly-crying into my Hot Cheetos? Also no. A tiny flicker of schadenfreude? Guilty as charged. Was it petty? Obviously. But after years of her theatrics, I'd earned the right to savor this like a Saint Honoré donut on a Sunday morning—flaky, indulgent, and best enjoyed without guilt.

And why shouldn't I? Tegan had swiped my boyfriend back when he still thought frosted tips were a personality. Sure, hindsight revealed he was about as appealing as a soggy fry left under a heat lamp, and yes, the trash had taken itself out. But it didn't erase the humiliation of being blindsided by someone I'd trusted like a bestie. So no, karma hadn't finished its shift yet, but damn, it felt good to watch her stilettos wobble.

Felicia's voice sliced through my thoughts, sharp as a sushi knife. "I say you steal Dick Print," she declared, sipping her wine like she'd just invented the concept of revenge. "Wouldn't that be *chef's kiss* perfection?"

A jolt of excitement shot down my spine, and I couldn't stop the grin spreading across my face. The idea was bonkers, ludicrous, and delightfully deranged—but it ignited a spark in me that had been hibernating. It wasn't about the guy—honestly, I'd struggle to ID him in a lineup unless he was holding a sign that read "Tegan's Upgrade." It was about the principle. The symmetry. The poetic justice of force-feeding Tegan a heaping spoonful of her own medicine.

"I could never," I blurted, the lie slipping out as

smoothly. But even as I said it, I could feel the idea taking root, sprouting vines of mischief. Imagining Tegan's face—a perfect blend of shock and rage—was already giving me the kind of joy usually reserved for finding a crumpled $20 in the wash.

Felicia snorted, unimpressed. "You can't let her win, Eva," she said, her tone a mix of cheerleader and dictator. "You're not the same girl who always let Tegan win anymore. You're Eva-fucking-Torres, and you don't take it lying down anymore."

A laugh erupted from somewhere deep, surprising me. "You really think I could pull it off?" I asked, half-joking, half-wondering if I'd accidentally swallowed a bravery potion.

She smirked, eyes glittering like she'd just hacked the Matrix. "Think? Baby, I know you can."

The words hung in the air, daring and absurd, and for a moment, I let myself daydream. Tegan's Botoxed smirk dissolving into horror. The cosmic scales tipping. The sweet, buttery taste of revenge, like a croissant baked with petty malice.

"Holy shit," I gasped, the realization hitting me like a lightning bolt. "I'm going to steal Tegan's boyfriend."

The words felt wild, electric, like swan-diving off a cliff with nothing but a prayer. It wasn't about him—it was about clawing back a shred of dignity, proving I wasn't the same girl who'd let Tegan treat her like a human welcome mat. I had no clue how to execute this masterplan, or if it was even possible, but for the first time in years, I felt *alive*.

Truly, unapologetically alive.

And honestly? It tasted better than a stolen sip of champagne at a dry wedding.

CHAPTER

FOUR

ONCE UPON A TIME, I'd had dreams.

Stupid dreams, but I'd had them. And it didn't consist of a revenge plot to steal a man, either.

Back when Tegan and I were still friends, we came up with this genius three-step plan to land our dream jobs—VIP bottle girls at the hottest nightclub in Vegas. We were young, full of ambition, and honestly, a little naive. But I was obsessed with the idea.

Tegan and I had it all figured out. We were going to rule the Strip, one overpriced bottle of champagne at a time. Our three-step plan was supposed to be foolproof, a masterpiece, really.

Step one, become lifeguards at the Palms Pool. Not to actually save lives (though the irony of us rescuing hungover tech bros was not lost on me). No, this was purely strategic.

The pool was where the rich, bored, and newly divorced congregated, and we'd flirt our way into their contact lists. Tegan once accidentally but not on accident dropped her sunscreen on a hedge fund guy's Louis Vuitton towel. He tipped her $300 to reapply it. On his back.

Step one had been a breeze. A walk in the park.

And coincidentally, the only step I'd completed.

Because, step two, had been to trade lifeguard whistles for sequined bikinis. We'd graduate to go-go dancing at Eclipse. Tegan had the legs of a gazelle who'd discovered Pilates, while I had the confidence of a girl who'd watched *Coyote Ugly* countless times. We'd shimmy, smile, and strategically forget to charge guys for their third Rum and Coke.

Networking, baby.

Step three, bottle service royalty. We'd wear dresses so tight they'd count as compression therapy, pour champagne for rappers who'd forget our names by sunrise, and rake in tips that could fund our inevitable retirement to a life of influencer-branded detox teas.

We'd daydream about it while slathering SPF 50 on tourists who'd clearly never heard of melanoma. "Accidentally spill a drink on a CEO," Tegan would say, "and he'll buy the whole bar out of guilt." I'd counter, "Or you'll *lose* your earring in a billionaire's pocket and he'll request you at his VIP table every time." We'd laugh and plan and daydream.

We were basically Ocean's 8, but with more sequins and little to no skill.

Then Tegan decided to pull a *Gossip Girl* twist and sabotage the entire operation.

It all started back at step one, with an intimidating manager and a missing tennis bracelet and blah blah blah, vibrating truck and all that. Suddenly, I was unemployed, blacklisted from every poolside gig in Vegas, and a reputation like that couldn't survive in a big small town like Vegas.

One minute, I was ready to shimmy my way to the top of Vegas, and the next I was standing there, blinking, wondering how the hell I ended up with nothing but a ruined reputation and a giant hole where my future used to be.

And Tegan didn't just swipe my job and my boyfriend. She took my sense of security, my three-step plan, and—because she's really thorough—she even took my faith in people. All in one fell swoop.

If you'd told twenty-four-year-old me that I'd end up working at a beige-walled medical office in a strip mall next to a discount tire shop and an H&R Block, I'd have laughed so hard I'd have fallen off my lifeguard stand. Yet here I was, four years deep into my role as the Do-It-All at Nondescript Medical, part injection-mixer, part Spanglish translator, part human paperweight for the mountain of insurance forms that never seemed to shrink.

Lifeguarding wasn't exactly glamorous, either. My thighs stuck to the plastic chair, my hair fried into a frizz ball under the Vegas sun, and I'd once had to fish a drunk bridesmaid's wig out of the pool. But back then, I'd had a plan, and plus, it had only been step one. A glitter-dusted, slightly delusional plan, but a plan nonetheless. Step one was supposed to be the grind; step two, the glow-up; step three, the money, honey! But instead, my life had stalled like a rusty pickup truck on the I-15, hazards blinking and all, while everyone else zoomed past.

Cali, my older sister and resident overachiever, had seen it coming way before I did. Cali'd said my plan was not a real plan and I needed to think about college and start getting serious about my future, but I always told her it wasn't for me. College was for Cali, for people who made pros and cons lists and volunteered at the local pet shelter. Still, she'd nagged me for years, her voice a mix of Big Sister Concern and Ivy League judgment. "College isn't just for people who like school, Eva. It's for people who don't want to end up…" She'd trail off, but I knew the end of that sentence… *"like*

Mom." Our mother, who'd worked two jobs her whole life and still couldn't afford to fix the AC or get me the new jeans everyone was wearing at school.

I'd shrug and blow her off, still believing in my delusions. "Some of us just want to live, you know? No five-year plans, no existential dread."

No five-year plans, indeed.

The medical office job had fallen into my lap three years ago when my roommate's cousin's girlfriend quit abruptly, and I'd clung to it like a life raft. The pay was steady, the hours predictable, and nobody accused me of stealing their Rolex. But some days, when I'd mixed my hundredth vial of cortisone or translated for the third time in my bad first-generation Spanish, I'd stare at the motivational cat poster in the break room ("Hang in there!") and wonder if this was really it.

"You have to meet my boyfriend tonight," Lexi announced, jolting me out of my latest existential crisis. She perched on a supply room stool, gloved hands mixing up a fresh batch of local anesthetic like it was a Cosmopolitan. "He's perfect. And—" she added, waggling a syringe like a fairy godmother's wand, "—his friends are all obscenely single. And rich. Obscenely rich, single friends."

Lexi was one of the six back-office girls at the clinic, a

title that made us sound like a 90s girl band, if the band's hits included "I Will Survive (This Paperwork)" and "Respect (My Personal Space, Dr. Greg)." She was a walking tornado of Louboutins, hair extensions that could double as a security blanket, and life choices that made my mother's experimental phase in LA look like a UN peace treaty.

Self-professed gold digger? Check. Master of flirting with men old enough to remember prohibition? Double check.

Yet somehow, she'd become my closest friend.

Maybe it was her ability to discuss Gucci handbags with the reverence of a TED Talk speaker. Or the fact she'd once tried to pay me in Chanel clutch for covering her shift. ("It's vintage, duh" she'd insisted, as if that explained everything.) The other girls stayed away from her, clutched their Starbucks lattes and whispered about 401(k)s, but I'd survived Tegan's betrayal and a three-step life plan that crashed harder than a middle-aged dude's Harley. Lexi's chaos was like ASMR for my mid-twenties meltdown.

"He's a businessman," she purred, flashing a smile so bright it could've powered the Strip. The kind of smile that made her look like she'd stepped out of a vintage magazine cover from the early 2000s. It wasn't just a smile, it was *the* smile—the one she'd mastered years ago, the one that made her look like she was one pout away from making millions.

She had perfected it, like a siren luring you into her world of old money, flashy cars, and endless luxuries. It was, of course, all a well curated act.

And I had to admit, she was almost *too* good at it. Lexi was essentially a modern-day Angelina Jolie—but not the Angelina we all know and love, the philanthropist, the great mom, Brad Pitt's fumble. No, she was the *early aughts* Angelina. The one with the full lips, the tousled hair, and that perfectly dangerous edge. Drop dead gorgeous, and completely alluring.

"I can't," I protested, slapping labels onto syringes like a factory robot. "Felicia needs a ride, and I'm… tired." Tired of rich men who think *generous* means paying for dinner and expecting a foot rub, that is.

Lexi's last boyfriend had been a septuagenerian sugar daddy with a neck wattle and a collection of vintage Rolexes. He'd spent our entire dinner interrogating me about my "low-paying job" while Lexi texted me under the table, "Play along, he's buying me a BMW!"

Lexi rolled her eyes, snapping off her gloves with a dramatic flourish. "Babe, *please*. His friends own penthouses. And one of them looks exactly like a young Hugh Grant. Pre-divorce, post-*Love Actually*."

I hesitated. Dangerously. "But Felicia—"

"Bring Felicia!" Lexi insisted, swirling vials of lidocaine. "We'll make it a girls' night! Well, sort of—Claire's nine months pregnant and currently Googling 'how to evict a tenant from my uterus,' so she's out. Heather's banned because she still hasn't returned my Dior clutch from Thanksgiving and plus, that other ting. And before you ask— no, I will *not* be taking questions at this time." She waved a syringe dismissively. "But Felicia's fun enough! Plus, I need you to meet him. He's different."

I arched a brow—a skill I'd perfected after six months of working with Lexi. "Different how? Last time you said that, your date turned out to be older than my father."

Her eyes sparkled. "Babe, you already know. He's *rich* rich. Not buys-you-a-McFlurry and wants to go halfsies. We're talking kinda sorta owns-a-private-island rich." She leaned in, her voice dropping to a whisper. "He's got a Rolex *and* more brown hair than white this time. It's like the universe finally did its homework. Hot, and generational wealth."

My gut screamed *run*. But then Tegan's smug face flashed in my mind with her shiny Tesla and Dick Print boyfriend. Meanwhile, here I was, labeling syringes and debating whether "more brown hair than white" meant dyed or natural.

"I don't know," I muttered, stabbing a needle into a vial. "Last time was like hanging with the Crypt Keeper. His friends kept asking if I needed help paying for college and winking like creeps."

Lexi snorted, snapping off her gloves like she was auditioning for *CSI: Las Vegas*. "That fossil? Please. This one's a *trust fund baby*. He's got a PhD in Hotness and a minor in Being Obnoxiously Charming."

"I thought he was a businessman."

"Yeah, well, there is no law that says he can't be both. Part-time business man, full-time heir to a golf course empire," she said, flipping her extensions with the drama of a Netflix finale. "Multitasking, darling. And I'm telling you, he has friends. Think *Succession*, but with better hair."

"Wait—the Mr. Darcy-looking one?"

She smirked, tossing her hair. "Ten p.m. at The Wynn. Be there, or be a freaking loser."

She vanished in a cloud of vanilla-chiffon perfume, leaving me slumped at my desk, glaring at the clinic's motivational poster. A thousand excuses bubbled up. *I have laundry! My cactus needs watering! I'm emotionally allergic to men in boat shoes!*

But then Tegan's laugh echoed in my head—that

polished, I've-stolen-your-life-and-made-it-sparkle laugh. She'd leap at a night like this. She'd probably already be there, flirting with a champagne flute and a well-known heir.

The possibilities were endless. What if I married rich? The fantasy unfurled like a TikTok montage: me, draped in couture I couldn't pronounce, sipping martinis on a yacht named Tax Write-Off, hash-tagging WifeyMaterial while Tegan seethed from her sparkling white Tesla parked outside the café.

I barked out a laugh, loud enough that Dr. Greg poked his head in, eyebrows raised. "Everything okay?"

"Peachy," I lied, shoving the syringe tray into the fridge.

But the idea clung like glitter. I could practically hear Tegan's sneer. *"You? A gold digger? You couldn't even dig up a coupon. Har har har."*

Yet here I was, mentally drafting a Bumble bio that screamed, "Looking for a man who knows the difference between Roth IRA and rosé." Pathetic? Maybe. But after years of watching Tegan win by playing dirty, maybe it was time to borrow her playbook.

Steal her man. Steal her life. Steal her spotlight.

I sighed, texting Felicia, "Mainline caffeine. We're hunting rich people."

I glanced at my reflection in the stainless-steel cabinet. My scrubs may be wrinkled, my ponytail a sad mess, but my eyeliner? Sharp enough to kill.

Game on, bitch.

CHAPTER

FIVE

"YOU CAN TAKE THE girl out of Vegas, but you can't take Vegas out of the girl," I muttered, smirking at my reflection as I dabbed on lip liner that promised Bombshell Drama! The phrase had lodged in my brain after a late-night trash TV binge, and tonight, as Felicia bounced in the living room of our shared apartment like a golden retriever in sequins, it felt weirdly prophetic.

"Okay, *fine*," I said, nervous like a girl at prom. "But if we're doing this, we're doing it properly. Lexi's Rules of Engagement, yeah?"

She leaned in, her big brown eyes wide with a mix of nerves and excitement, like a kid about to ride a roller coaster for the first time. "Lay it on me, Girl Boss."

I cringed. "That's not—"

"No, you're right," she backtracked. "Too cringy."

Channeling Lexi's chaotic energy (and her questionable morals), I held up a finger. "Rule One: You're the CEO of this interaction. If he wants access to the Golden Globes—" I gestured vaguely at her sequined top, "—he invests. No free samples. Got it?"

"Got it," she said, nodding so vigorously her hoop earrings chimed. "I'm a luxury girl. Limited edition."

"Rule Two: Play mysterious and coy," I continued. "Laugh at his jokes, but like… ironically. If he mentions tech, say 'Darling, I only invest in diamonds and trauma.' Keep him guessing."

Felicia mimed taking notes. "Mystery. Got it. What's Rule Three?"

"Rule three: Always order the priciest thing on the menu. Champagne, caviar, whatever. If he balks, he's not worth your time. This is about making him pay—literally—for your company."

She fist-pumped. "I was born to bankrupt a man!"

I hesitated, Lexi's voice hissing in my head like banshee. "Rule Four—the holy grail: Do. Not. Go. Home. With. Him. Even if he says he owns a yacht and a vineyard. Even if he has a full head of hair."

Felicia's nose scrunched. "But what if he's perfect? What

if he's… Pedro Pascal?"

"Especially then!" I groaned, recalling Lexi's "Never trust a man who looks good" lecture. "Men with good hair and money have nothing to lose. You'll end up his quirky anecdote at brunch with his ex-wife's barre group."

She scrunched her face. "I can't do anything, then. I might as well be in the cast of *Jane the Virgin*."

I sighed—the kind of sigh usually reserved for delayed planes and self-checkout machines that yell "unexpected item in bagging area"—and pinched the bridge of my nose like I was trying to erase the last hour. "Felicia, for the last time. If you go home with him tonight, he'll think he's won the lottery without buying a ticket. Next thing you know, he'll be ghosting you faster than a 7-Eleven 3-for-1 deal disappears on a hungover Sunday. *Then* where's that Birkin bag you offhandedly mentioned? Or that penthouse he definitely promised after three G&Ts?"

She crossed her arms, pouting like a toddler denied a Hershey's Kiss. "But what if he's, like, obscenely fine?"

"Then you make him woo you like you're the last Twinkie in the packet!" I said, slinging my Nordstrom Rack tote over my shoulder, ready to get this night over with. "Dinner dates. Show tickets. A penthouse on the Strip. That's gold-digging 101, Felicia." Nerves prickled the palms of my hands. "If not, then you might as well date a Tinder swipe who'll bitch and moan about furnishing your shared studio apartment with IKEA furniture. Lexi didn't earn her BMW by taking the man home on the first date."

Felicia blinked, processing this as if I'd asked her to explain global warming. "Oh," she said finally. "So it's like regular dating, but with more steps?" To be fair, she wasn't that thick. She was just excited about finally having a night out.

"Exactly," I said, ushering her out the door. "Now, let's go get us some trust fund babies."

We scurried to my car—the same gaudy neon green one—and transformed from "medical assistant and barista" to "sirens of mild debauchery" using eyeliner, Shein sequins, and sheer delusion. As we sped toward the Wynn, the seven-year-old car wheezing, I white-knuckled the steering wheel. "What if this backfires?" I muttered. "What if we end up on a milk carton?"

I glanced at Felicia. She was scrolling Instagram, neon pink nails tapping like Morse code for "I have no survival instincts."

"Aren't you nervous?" I asked.

"Nah," she said, blotting her lipstick with a Taco Bell napkin. "Worst case, we get free champagne and a story for the ages."

Then, like a plot twist, she gasped. "Wait—doesn't Lexi sleep with her sugar daddy?"

I rolled my eyes so hard I nearly reversed into a Smart Car. "Lexi's been with him for a year. He's funded her entire existence, including that lip filler she claims is 'just good genes.' It's a career, Felicia. Not a quickie behind a Wendy's."

"Fine," she huffed, tossing her silky curls. "No quickies. Unless he's literally Henry Cavill. Or… a sad Henry Cavill. Like, post-breakup, owns a puppy Henry Cavill."

"No," I said, channeling my inner high school principal. "Repeat. The. Rules."

She groaned, as if I'd asked her to recite the Pledge of Allegiance. "Rule one: Flirt like I'm in a *Bridgerton* spin-off. Rule two: Order the most expensive thing on the menu— even if it's snails. Rule three: No. Quickies. Unless he's…"

"No."

"…wearing a kilt?"

"Felicia."

"Fine," she said, grinning. "But if he looks like Pedro Pascal, I'm texting you 'codeword: guacamole.'"

I laughed, despite the existential dread. "Just stick to the plan. And if anyone asks, we're heiresses to a... uh... artisanal raw milk empire."

"Got it," she said, fluffing her curls. "Farmer queens."

As the rain streaked past the window of my wheezing car (which smelled vaguely of stale fries), my mind drifted to Tegan. Where was she now? Likely draped over a Chesterfield sofa in some Summerlin townhouse, sipping Veuve Clicquot with her Dick Print boyfriend, giggling about how she'd "accidentally" stolen my job, my ex, and my favorite Zara coat. Meanwhile, I was playing Eliza Doolittle to Felicia's Vivian Ward—if Vivian's goal was to bag a hedge funder with a questionable hairline and a yacht named Tax Evasion.

A simmering resolve had been brewing since the day I'd bumped into Tegan outside the café, her new Louis Vuitton tote conveniently grazing my Marc Jacobs dupe. Then, it was a mere spark of indignation. Now? A full-blown inferno, stoked by every "Oh, Eva, you're still the same," shrill reminder. I was done letting her squat in my psyche like a student tenant refusing to move out.

"Time to Marie Kondo this mess," I muttered, white-knuckling the steering wheel. "Sparks joy, my ass."

Felicia glanced up from contouring her cheeks with a

e.l.f. highlighter. "What?"

"Nothing. Just marveling at how this'll either be genius or a Netflix documentary."

She squealed, kicking her glittery H&M heels against the dashboard. "Trust fund babies, brace yourselves!"

I snorted, the car hiccuping as we passed a lit-up Wynn parking. Its glow mirrored Felicia's highlighter—garish yet weirdly compelling.

"Oh! Saw Dick Print today," Felicia added, faux-casual. "Ordered two cappuccinos. One for Teflon Tegan, no doubt."

My stomach lurched like the time I'd accidentally liked my ex's engagement post. "Fantastic. Preferred them when they were at each other's throats."

"Same. But chin up! Tonight, we bag a man who at least knows what good champagne is."

"Aim high," I deadpanned, swerving into the self-park.

As we neared the Wynn, its awning dripping with Vegas drizzle and misplaced hopes, an odd calm settled over me. This wasn't the three-step plan I'd daydreamed at the Palms lifeguarding. But it was my life, and I'd take it.

"Okay," I said, double-parking with the confidence of someone who'd never paid a parking ticket. "Let's go charm a man who unironically says 'Tab on my Black Amex.'"

Felicia fist-pumped, her clutch spilling gummy bears. "Operation *Bridgerton* But Cynical is a go!"

And with that, we teetered into the lobby, ready to rewrite the rules of romance—or at least expense a glass or two of Dom Pérignon.

CHAPTER

SIX

❧

"EVA!" LEXI's VOICE SLICED through the thumping bass like a plane through a cloud. We were wedged at the entrance of XS Nightclub, Vegas' answer to existential dread, where Lexi clung to the arm of a flushed, middle-aged man in a suit that cost more than my student loans. The line behind us snaked halfway down the casino—a glittering parade of spray tans, $30 cocktails, and influencers yelling "POV: You're missing out!" into their phones. Lexi merely fluttered her lashes at the bouncer, a man built like a box of Twinkies. "Darling," she trilled, nodding at him, "they're with me."

Felicia and I swapped a look—half mortified, half giddy—as the bouncer unhooked the velvet rope. Lexi air-kissed my cheek, her vanilla-cherry perfume mingling with the scent of desperation and stolen cigars. "We never wait, silly," she said, as if this were a universal truth, like "brunch solves everything" or "all men lie." Her dress, a leopard-print

65

contraption, clung to her like cellophane, channeling peak *I'm here to steal your husband and your Spanx* energy.

"Meet Charles," she announced, draping herself over him like a cashmere throw. "My favorite trust fund baby."

And while Charles may very well have a trust fund, a baby he most certainly was not.

His ruddy cheeks deepened to merlot, his combover quivering under the strobe lights. He had the soft, doughy look of a man who'd never missed a dessert cart in his life, his champagne belly testing the limits of his Burberry shirt. Salt-and-pepper stubble dusted his jaw—more salt, honestly—and his laugh sounded like a wheezy accordion. But Lexi gazed up at him like he'd personally saved a baby bird, her fingers toying with his gold Rolex.

Felicia elbowed me, shouting over a remix of a popular song that now sounded like a robot apocalypse. "He looks like he's never made his own bed. And old enough to be from the time before beds were even a thing!"

I bit my lip to stop laughing. Gold-digging had seemed so simple over a bottle of Trader Joe's $6 rosé. Now? I was sweating like a pig at a luau.

Lexi, meanwhile, was in her natural habitat—a panther in Louboutins, hunting prey with a Black Amex. "Charles loves this song," she purred, though the track was just "YMCA" remixed with dubstep. She nibbled his earlobe. "Don't you, sweetheart?"

"Y-yes!" Charles barked, spilling his whisky. "Reminds me of… Ibiza 2003!"

"Chop-chop!" Lexi herded us toward a roped-off booth where a server was already pouring Dom Pérignon into glasses taller than Felicia's boots. "Eva, unclench. You look like you're at your yearly gyno appointment."

"I'm fine!" I lied, my smile tighter than her Spanx.

She thrust a coupe into my hand, the bubbles tickling my nose like liquid audacity. "Drink. Flirt. Pretend you've never heard the word *dignity*."

I gulped the champagne, its dryness burning away my moral high ground. "I'm here, aren't I?"

Lexi's grin widened. "There's hope for you yet."

As the champagne fizzed in my stomach like a packet of Pop Rocks, I couldn't shake the feeling I'd time-travelled back to my three-step life plan era. The bass thumped against my ribs like a disgruntled Uber driver, and neon lights strobed across the dance floor like a filter gone rogue. A flicker of déjà vu prickled my skin—until Lexi's laugh cut through the noise, sharp as a CVS receipt and twice as glittery.

Lexi flourished, of course. While I mentally drafted my resignation letter to the Moral High Ground Committee, she moved through the chaos like she'd been born in it—utterly unbothered. And okay, fine, older men weren't *all* bad. George Clooney? Adorable. Colin Firth in *Bridget Jones's Baby*? A national treasure. But Lexi's taste leaned less silver fox and more Anna Nicole Smith's Inheritance Era. Still, Charles—with his combover clinging for dear life and a belly that screamed *give me champagne*—was a marked improvement from her last beau: a leathery septuagenarian who called his Porsche "the other woman" and Lexi "the weekend hobby." Progress, I supposed.

"Ladies!" Lexi bellowed, flinging her arms wide enough to knock over a tower of Ferrero Rocher. "Welcome to your kingdom!" She planted a kiss on Charles's cheek, leaving a lipstick stain. "You're amazing, baby. Thank you for tonight."

Charles puffed out his chest, his Burberry shirt straining. "Anything for my queen."

Felicia choked on her champagne, snorting into her glass.

I sank into the booth, the leather sticking to my thighs like a bad Tinder swipe, and scanned the room. It was the same gilded circus I'd sworn off years ago—back when I thought "networking" meant laughing at a banker's *Wolf of Wall Street* impressions. The women still sparkled like disco balls at a 2016 office party, the men still reeked of Tom Ford and unearned confidence, and the air still hummed with the desperation of someone who'd maxed out their Amex.

"Bottoms up, bitches!" Lexi shouted, hoisting her glass so high I worried she'd dislocate a shoulder. Champagne sloshed precariously, but she didn't care. She turned to Charles, hips swaying, and began grinding against him.

But I'd vowed to enjoy tonight. Even if "enjoy" meant surviving Ty, Charles's friend who now loomed over Felicia like a lamppost in a Tom Ford suit. And Scott—salt-and-pepper hair, a grin suggesting he'd invested in his teeth, and a cologne that screamed "hello!"—extended a shaky hand to me. "Scott," he wheezed, minty breath battling the cologne for dominance. "Shall we… boogie?"

Boogie. The word hung in the air like a bad smell. I glanced at Felicia, now trapped in a conversation with Ty, a man whose stature screamed #2 pencil, and forced a smile. "Why not?"

As Scott shuffled toward the dance floor, Lexi shot me a wink. "Live a little, darling!" she mouthed, draped over Charles like a Gucci scarf.

I sighed, eyeing the exit. Maybe tonight wasn't about gold-digging. Maybe it was about remembering why I'd traded VIP sections for early nights and free cortados.

"He keeps calling me 'kitten,'" Felicia hissed, clutching my arm like I was the last thing holding her to reality. "I'd rather be at home watching *Gilmore Girls* in my Shein pajamas."

"Same," I whispered back. "But at least the drinks are free."

We'd come tonight out of curiosity—and mild peer pressure from Lexi, who'd texted, *"Ur 30 now babe. Last chance 2 be delulu!"* Even though she was the one who was thirty, and I was only twenty-eight. But as Scott droned on about his exotic vacation "mansion" in Hawaii, it hit me. Growth isn't just switching from vodka Red Bulls to herbal tea. It's realizing that this—the sticky floors, the forced giggles, the men who think generational wealth is a personality—isn't a flex. It's a *Snapped* episode waiting to happen.

"Remember when we thought bottle service was peak adulthood?" I muttered, eyeing a wobbling champagne tower.

"Peak delusion, more like," Felicia snorted. "Though I wouldn't say no to stealing these napkins. They're nicer than the café towels."

But as Felicia and I clinked glasses—silently agreeing to flee after one more round—I felt a weird pride. I'd dipped my toes back into the chaos, and guess what? The water was foul.

"To surviving," I said, raising my glass.

"To escaping," Felicia corrected, nodding at Ty, who was now attempting a dad dance to Dua Lipa.

Felicia squinted at the menu like it was written in hieroglyphics. "What's the most expensive thing here? Something that screams, 'I summer in Saint-Tropez but also have to show it off'?"

I skimmed the list, choking on my the prices. I thought $30 cocktails were bad. "The Ono cocktail is ten bands. Served with a side of privilege."

Her eyes lit up like a winning slot machine. "*Perfect*. Let's bankrupt these dudes. Tastefully, of course."

Across the table, Lexi had transformed into a human limpet, suctioned to Charles' side. "Babyyyy," she purred, feeding him a truffle fry like it was ambrosia, "get us more drinks. Top-shelf only—or I'll have to tell Pussy Cat you've been naughty." She pouted, her gloss shimmering like a traffic cone. "Eva wants the Ono cocktail. And hurry—the ice in my veins is melting."

I waved my hands to get her attention and flashed two fingers, mouthing, "Felicia too."

Lexi winked. "Make it three, darling. I'm parched."

Charles, sweating through his Burberry shirt like an iced tea in the South, nodded wildly. "Anything for my queen!"

It was almost art, the way Lexi puppeteered him. If she'd demanded his vintage Aston Martin, he'd have tossed her the keys and thrown in his ex-wife's Spanx.

Scott, my "date" and walking argument for prohibition, lurched over, smelling like a strip club after-hours. "Eva! Dance with me, you *vision*!" he bellowed, spittle landing on my lap.

"Waiting on my Ono," I shouted back, dodging his champagne-breath.

He leaned in, minty desperation wafting off him. "I'll buy you The Forum Shops, sweet thing! The whole damn floor!"

"Ooh, The Forum," I gasped, sidestepping his grabby hands. "Do they do returns?"

Felicia, meanwhile, was fending off Ty with an empty coupe and a glare sharper than shards of glass. So much for taking him home.

"Gotta pee!" I announced, fleeing toward the toilets, Felicia clacking behind me.

The bathroom was a a sanctuary of flickering lights and a sign that read "Don't Flush Your Dreams." We collapsed against the sinks, howling like hyenas on a bender.

"This is a disaster," Felicia wheezed, mascara bits cascading down her cheeks.

"A beautiful disaster," I corrected, blotting lipstick with a Chipotle napkin. "But free ten band drinks, babe."

She snorted. "Let's just survive this night, yeah. I'm ready to go back to regular life."

Back in the fray, Lexi was now throned on Charles' lap, feeding him grapes like a Roman empress. Scott waved, his combover defying gravity like a Starlink gone bad.

I was beginning to feel good, to let myself enjoy the fruits of my labor as the top shelf alcohol settled in, making me more comfortable around Scott. I even scooted a little closer to hear him over the thumping bass of the club, letting my guard down, thinking that a Chanel purse wouldn't be so bad to get out of this, would it.

"Drinks are here," Lexi trilled, as a bottle girl neared with our ridiculously normal looking but very expensive drinks.

And then—

My heart dropped to my knees.

Tegan.

Years. It had been years since I'd seen her. And now here she was, gliding into the VIP section like Megan Markle at a charity. In this very nightclub. In the same VIP section where the whispers of what was really going on were louder than the music.

She locked eyes with me, her smirk widening as she clocked Scott's combover, Ty's cologne cloud, and Lexi hand-feeding Charles a bundle of grapes dipped in gold leaf.

"Oh. My. God," Felicia whispered, clutching my arm. "Is that—"

Tegan glided toward our area, a tray of overpriced cocktails gleaming under the strobe lights. My pulse raced as I shrank into my seat, desperately hoping the neon glow would swallow me whole.

Lexi, oblivious, was mid-rant about Charles' *alarming tongue technique* when she chirped, "Thanks, babe! Love the Onos!"

Of course she's the bottle girl. VIP, too!

Tegan flashed Lexi a smile polished by years of stealing my joy. "Anytime, babe," she purred, her eyes darting to me like a wasp spotting a jam sandwich.

I turned to Felicia, whispering hoarsely, "She's the *bottle girl*?!"

"The bottle girl!" Felicia hissed back, nearly upending her 10k Ono.

"Fuck," I muttered, watching Tegan sashay off, hips swaying to the beat.

Felicia buried her face in her hands. "I'll never recover from this. I'm moving to St. George. Changing my name. Learning crochet."

Across the booth, Scott's hand slithered toward my waist. "Eva, sweetness—"

"Bathroom!" I barked, lurching upright. "Again!"

Felicia vaulted over Ty's loafers. "Same! Urgently!"

"Hey, where are you guys going?"

"Gotta go!" I called out, dismissing Lexi with a wave of hand.

"It's okay," Lexi yelled out quickly, trying to smooth things over with the older men. "They're boring anyway! I have other girlfriends coming that are way more fun than they are! Oh, and these drinks," she said, chugging an Ono at once, "are all mine!"

A little pang of regret hit me, thinking maybe I could've had my drink before leaving. But I stuck to my resolve and just muttered a half-hearted, "Good!" over my shoulder as I moved faster, practically sprinting toward the exit.

We bolted, heels clacking like castanets, but Tegan materialized in our path, tray aloft. Sparklers fizzed on her cocktails, illuminating her smirk brighter than New Years Eve fireworks at the Strip.

Our eyes locked. Hers said, *You're dancing with Combover Ken while I'm out here* slaying. Mine said, *I will* end *you with this dupe tote.*

Felicia yanked me past her. "Later, hate-sparkle," she tossed over her shoulder.

Outside, Vegas drizzle slapped some sense into us.

"Well," Felicia said, fishing a half-squashed gold-leafed grape bunch from her purse, "that was…"

"A disaster," I finished, popping the car open, wishing I'd ordered an Uber instead. "But at least Lexi got her BMW fund topped up."

"Small mercies," she agreed.

As we slumped into the car—which smelled faintly of regret—Felicia groaned, "I'm never going to be able to look Dick Print in the eye again." Followed by, "Do you think Lexi's still feeding Charles grapes?"

"Undoubtedly. She downed those Ono drinks, too. Damn

her."

We dissolved into giggles, the kind that bubble up when you've narrowly escaped being a documentary subject.

"Sober?" Felicia asked, the thought of driving after drinks just now hitting her too.

"Sharp as a tack," I said.

"In-N-Out?" Felicia suggested.

"Grilled onions and extra cheese," I said. "And no men over 35."

"Deal."

As we licked sauce from our fingers later, I realized: Tegan could keep her sparklers and smugness. I had a Desert Bloom loyalty card, a best friend, and a very detailed plan to "accidentally" spill coffee on her tomorrow.

CHAPTER
SEVEN

WAKING UP FRESH AND early on a Saturday used to feel like a personal offense to my entire generation. In my early twenties, it meant I'd tragically missed a 3 a.m. karaoke rendition of "I Will Survive" or failed to secure greasy midnight tacos that could double as a skincare routine. Now, at the ripe old age of twenty-eight? It felt like winning the Olympics of Adulthood or like I'd wake up to receive a participation award for Not The Most Responsible Adult, But She's Trying category. Especially after last night's catastrophe, which I'd rank somewhere between forgetting my pants on a Zoom call and accidentally liking my ex's wedding photos.

The night had been a masterclass in humiliation—a parade of geriatric trust-fund babies, a dance floor encounter with a man whose hips creaked louder than my IKEA bed frame, and Tegan. Tegan, who'd materialized like a Botoxed specter from my past, smirking as she served 10K cocktails with a side of schadenfreude. By the time I'd face-planted into bed, I half-expected Netflix to option the horror show as Cringe: The Musical.

But today I'd conquered Pilates, and at 7 a.m., too. I'd rolled out of bed, wrestled into leggings that promised a bum lift (delivered), and marched to the studio like a warrior queen. Forty-five minutes of reformer hell later and I'd sweat out last night's shame. Take *that*, universe.

Parking my car—the seven year-old gaudy green thing—I scanned for Tegan's Tesla, a sleek monstrosity that screamed, *I can afford a car payment and you can't, Eva!* The coast was clear. Victory.

Striding into Desert Bloom Café, with a pep in my step, I felt redeemed. The scent of espresso and ambition wrapped around me like a hug. Felicia was somewhere in the back, flour in her hair and a glazed look in her eyes, regret eating her up, probably. Gone were her law school days of rigid routines and Pilates weekends—now she lived by the mantra, "Baking is chaos, and chaos pays the bills."

Cat Power crooned over the speakers, a soothing balm until I spotted Shane, the barista, locked in a standoff with a woman wielding a macchiato like a weapon.

"This isn't a macchiato!" she hissed. "Where's the

caramel? The separation? The drizzle?"

Shane, muttered, "This *is* a macchiato. It's espresso 'marked' with milk. The Starbucks version is basically a milkshake with a caffeine badge—"

"Unacceptable!" she barked, slamming the cup down. "I want a manager!"

I sidled up, grinning. "Manager's busy. She's got a croissant emergency in the back."

Shane huffed, snatching the macchiato back with a muttered, "Sure—let me just fix your mess."

"Oat milk cortado and that raspberry tart, please," I called out to him, slumping against the counter like a hungover student at a UNLV cafeteria.

Felicia burst from the kitchen, her auburn curls bouncing like she'd landed a shampoo ad. "Babe," she gasped, "thought you'd be face-down in bed today! Did you see the state of that VIP server's YSL heels last night? Looked like they'd been through a car wash." She meant the one before Tegan. She'd been nice, if a little messy.

Felicia's grin was infectious. Post-disaster mornings were weird like that—like surviving a bachelorette and waking up weirdly refreshed. Felicia looked radiant, mind. Skin dewy as a waxed apple, despite likely surviving on three hours of sleep and twelve espresso shots.

"Needed a treat after last night's meltdown," I said, swiping the tart. "Plus, Pilates was dead without your dramatic plank collapses."

"Ugh, don't mention Pilates," Felicia groaned, glancing around like she'd just remembered she left the oven on. "I miss it the most."

"At least your ass still looks tight."

She cackled, the sound warm as an old fireplace. "You're crazy. I'd still be in bed watching *Housewives* on repeat." She looked around again. "And no, I haven't seen Teflon Tegan today, so we're safe. Probably off getting her roots dyed to match her personality."

The café hummed with Saturday chaos—babies crying, Shane arguing with patrons, guys talking about football—but Felicia's eyes sparkled like she had a secret from the gossip column. I leaned in, nosey as a neighbor peering through curtains.

She smirked, lowering her voice. "Guess."

I followed her behind the counter, dodging a tray of muffins. "What?"

"Nosferatu's here."

I froze, brain buffering. Nosferatu—our nickname for the

guy who looked like he'd been kept in a Tupperware since 2007. Pale as a vampire, allergic to sunlight, and always ordering his coffee whiter than a MAGA conference. I scanned the room. "Where?"

"Bathroom. But he'll be back," she whispered, like the CIA had bugged the muffin tray. "When he comes, look at his eyes. Very dodgy. Swear to god, he's got that 'I know where you live' vibe."

I arched a brow. "What'd he say this time?"

"Told me I 'belong in a Parisian patisserie' and that my bakes 'remind him of his childhood in Provence.'" She fake-gagged. "Bet he's never even seen a baguette that wasn't from Costco."

I snorted. "Sounds almost romantic. Could've been worse," I said, recalling the time he'd told Felicia her curls belonged "under a bonnet in a Brontë novel."

"Oh, it got worse. Then he said my 'milk chocolate skin' looked 'sun-kissed' and he'd 'like to taste it.'"

Last night's champagne threatened a comeback. "*Jesus*— that's—"

"He's coming," she hissed, shooing me toward a table. "Sit. Now."

Working at Guy's café was leagues weirder than my

medical office gig. At least there, the most chaotic thing was a toddler chucking Tylenol at the receptionist. Here? Every regular's a walking *2 Broke Girls* reject. But Nosferatu? King of the creeps.

I watched him shuffle out, umbrella up like he'd melt in the Mojave sun—which, given his pallor, wasn't entirely implausible. He nodded at Felicia with all the charm of soggy bread, lingered just a tad too long, then caught his umbrella on the doorframe. *Bye, Dracula.*

Felicia exhaled like she'd been holding her breath since 2016, then vanished into a cloud of steam and passive aggression.

Bookless and bored, I slumped into my usual corner—the one with the wonky chair that screams *one bad move and it's over, bitch*—and doom-scrolled TikTok. The café's buzz faded to white noise… until a voice cut through like a knife through butter.

"Excuse me—don't I know you?"

I glanced up. *Oh. Fuck.*

There he stood. Dick Print. Two doors down. *That* Dick Print.

His eyes locked onto mine. Jawline stubbled like he'd meant to forget his razor. Cheekbones sharp enough to slice a watermelon. I swallowed. Hard.

Shit.

Tegan'd definitely told him about last night. The VIP section. The trust-fund what's-it's. Me grinding on a man old enough to remember the *actual* Nosferatu release. My face flamed hotter than a Cheeto.

Not that *he'd* care. Probably too busy being disgustingly fit and emotionally unavailable. But *I* cared. Enough to want to throw myself into the Bellagio fountain.

"Ohmygod—hi!" I squeaked, voice cracking like a X Factor reject.

He smiled. Dimples. *Dimples.* I died. Resurrected. Died again.

"Alright?" he said, smile warm enough to defrost a Costco freezer aisle. No judgement, no side-eye—just a guy who looked like he'd been carved from a *GQ* spread. His eyes—navy, like a pissed-off sea in an Alaskan cruise—crinkled at the corners, and *Jesus*, I was grinning back like a Labrador offered a pup cup. He smelled like fresh soap, and for a second, I forgot I'd mortified myself just hours earlier.

Dammit.

"Never better," I answered.

If Tegan knew I was here, batting eyelashes at her Dick

Print, she'd hex me via group chat. And if this man knew about last night's VIP disaster, I'd need to fake my death and move to St. George with Felicia.

"Never got your name the other day," he said, voice smooth and deep, and just the right intonation. "You yelled at me and booked it like a running back."

I laughed, my neck doing an impression of *The Exorcist*. "I was pulled away, if I remember correctly."

Nodding, he smiled a damning smile. "Right."

I inhaled sharply, channeling my inner cool girl. "Eva. Eva Torres."

"Eva Torres," he repeated, like he was savoring it. "Eric Mann." He held out a hand—rough, strong, manly—and I shook it. His grip was firm, warm, and *oh*, there it was, that fizzy *uh oh* spark. Dangerous. Delicious. Daring.

"Pleasure," I managed, voice wobblier than Jell-O. I attempted Lexi's signature effortless siren smirk, but honestly? Felt more like a 'I've eaten three Twinkies in the bathroom' grimace.

Especially because I'd resolved to swipe him from Tegan. As in, at that very moment, I'd decided. Casual *Game of Thrones* villain behavior. Tegan would've combusted on the spot, all filler and fury. But hey—if she could nab my ex (a guy with the charisma of a wet rag), why shouldn't I return the favor?

"Tegan mentioned you," he said, casually inserting her name in the conversation. "But she's… Tegan. Wouldn't introduce us. So here I am—tracking down her cute friend myself."

Cute? The word hit me like a champagne cork to the face.

But then again… since when did I play nice anymore?

"We *used* to know each other," I said, letting the bitterness leak out—all the while remembering this was *her* man. "She's a lot, you know?" The words tumbled free, unfiltered as a city council Twitter rant. But hell—he was still Tegan's man. Loyalty-bound. If I wanted to pull this off, I needed subtlety. Finesse. Tact. Channel my inner Lexi.

He smirked, all dimples and danger. "Thought you two were closer than that."

Felicia, bless her no-filter soul, chimed in like an open karaoke mic, "Eva hates her."

"Felicia!" I hissed, face flaming hotter than the worst sunburn.

"What?" She shrugged, like she'd just commented on the weather. "She's a bore. Everyone knows it."

My cheeks could've powered the whole Strip.

"Okay—Thanks for the coffee!" I blurted, fake-smiling so hard my cheeks ached. "Better check on those muffins—"

Felicia sauntered off, tossing Eric a wink. *Traitor.*

"She's funny," Eric said, voice like a velvet tracksuit.

"Lots of laughs," I muttered, praying for a sudden sinkhole. My nerves fizzed. Small talk. *Do small talk.* "So, you're here a lot, then?"

"Best cappuccino this side of the I-15." He kept chatting, but I was too busy mentally tracing his jawline—that stubble, the tiny mole on his chin. *Focus, Eva.*

"Crazy, right?" he said, snapping me back.

Dammit. What'd he say? "Uh-huh," I agreed, nodding like a bobblehead.

"Greg's leg snapped clean in two. You see that roundhouse?"

Fight? Oh *right*—UFC. Tegan'd mentioned he was some cage-fighting Adonis. Should've Googled. "Broke his leg? Yikes."

"Thought you said you watched it."

"Did," I lied, sweating like a grilled cheese. "Just… shut my eyes at that part. Like a wuss."

He laughed, warm and low. "Fair. It was pretty grim."

I sipped my coffee, brain screaming *stalk his Insta later!*

"It was brutal," Eric muttered, scrubbing a hand over his stubble like he was trying to erase the memory. "Guy's got months of therapy ahead. Now they're scouting replacements for his next match." He shrugged, his biceps flexing under his gym hoodie. "Thought about putting my name in, but…"

But you're too busy being distractingly handsome and tragically attached to Satan's handmaiden, I thought, nodding sympathetically. Why was he here, anyway, dissecting UFC drama with me over a cap, instead of with Tegan? Unless last night's VIP debacle had left her bed bound with karma-induced flu. The image of her smirking while balancing sparklers on a tray flashed in my mind, and I nearly scalded myself with my own saltiness.

"Sooo," Felicia chirped in, dropping off a refill. "Where's Tegan? Recovering from her grueling shift flirting with octogenarians?"

Felicia. I kicked her under the table. She yelped, then barreled on. "Saw you two arguing yesterday."

Eric's jaw twitched. "Tegan's… intense."

Felicia gasped, as if he'd confessed to smuggling truffles. "Intense. Right. Like a—"

"Thank you, Felicia," I hissed, shooing her toward a customer eyeing the almond croissants.

Eric stood, suddenly eager to leave. "Well, I better get back. Cardio waits for no man."

"Of course!" I chirped, channeling the calm of someone who hadn't just plotted home wrecking over a raspberry tart. "Send Tegan my love!"

He paused, brow furrowed like I'd asked him to explain the tax system. "Uh. Sure." Probably knew we hated each other. Oh well.

As he left, Felicia materialized behind me. "Do you think Tegan's told him we're a couple of gold diggers?"

"We're not a couple of gold diggers," I snapped, ignoring the twinge of guilt.

"She doesn't know that."

"She definitely told him."

She patted my shoulder. "Relax. If anyone's the villain here, it's her. Now, about Operation Steal Him—"

"It's not an operation," I lied, watching Eric's retreating form. God, even his walk was annoyingly perfect.

"Please. You've got that look."

"What look?"

"The one where you're mentally rehearsing meet-cutes in the Whole Foods salad aisle."

I scowled. "I'm strategizing. It's karma with a little push."

Felicia snorted. "Karma's been on vacation. Just promise me one thing."

"What?"

"If you do steal him, make sure he's got a friend. Preferably rich. And with a pulse."

We shared a laugh, the plan already unraveling in my head. But as Tegan's laugh echoed from the gym two doors down—sharp, polished, infuriating—something hardened in me.

A steel resolve.

It was about damned time.

CHAPTER
EIGHT

IT IS A TRUTH UNIVERSALLY known by anyone who's done their time in the health industry that it sucks.

Royally. Capital-S Sucks.

Anyone who says otherwise is either delusional or maybe they've got some kind of god complex—a hero complex, perhaps? Maybe some sort of Munchausen syndrome, some by-proxy ailment, to be sure.

And trust me, I'd know.

After my years spent lifeguarding at the Palms pool that smelled perpetually of chlorine and despair, I'd dreamt my twenties would be all rooftop bars and #LivingMyBestLife. Instead, Tegan took off with our three-step plan while I got stuck playing Tetris with specimen jars and explaining to senior citizens why we're out of hemorrhoid cream *again*. She climbed the ladder in stilettos; I tripped into a *Call the*

Midwife montage, minus the adorable babies. And let's not kid ourselves—her single night's tips probably covered my monthly rent.

These thoughts nipped at me during my morning routine. But what was I gonna do? Quit? Join the unemployment line with my impressive skills in hemorrhoid logistics? Hard pass.

"I'm really mad at you, you know," Lexi announced, slicing through the exam room's silence like a scalpel. I fumbled the glove box, sending latex flying. She'd been frosty all morning, her usual siren-like sparkle replaced with a villainous glare.

"Look, I'm sorry I ditched you at the club," I said, abandoning the gloves. "But schmoozing trust-fund babies? Not my vibe."

While Tegan hustled, Lexi's masterplan was classic rags to riches—bagging a rich guy, quit her job, and live off his Hamptons estate. Fair play—just not my jam. Not that I *had* a jam. Unless existential dread counts, and working for pennies like a dumb dumb.

"You didn't just ditch me," Lexi snapped, arms folded. "You took Felicia too. Left me juggling three men who thought banter meant quoting *Cheers*. Do you know how hard it is pretending to care about fucking *Cheers*? I had to call in reinforcements."

She slouched against the doorframe—a skill only Lexi could make look like a *Vogue* spread. Even livid, she oozed that Angelina bombshell aura.

I winced. "Really sorry, Lex. Should've said I'd rather club in Crocs. Who'd you call?"

Her glare sharpened. *Uh-oh.*

"…Heather?" I ventured. "The one who tried to swipe that hedge fund guy from you?"

Lexi rolled her eyes so hard I worried they'd stick. "Tried? She did! Which is why I'm fuming. That skank stole my man *and* my bag. Unforgivable."

She huffed, but we both knew her rage had the lifespan of McDonald's chicken nuggets left in the back of the car. Lexi's soft spot for me was Sphere huge—even if she'd sooner admit to owning Shein panties.

"Of course," she added, tone shifting from epic showdown to mildly entertained, "turns out the old geezer was a lying sack of potatoes. Scammed *her* instead. How's that for a karmic mic drop?"

"What?" I blinked. "You said he was loaded! Loaded enough to fund a *Marrying Millions* spin-off!"

I shook my head, baffled. Lexi was the human equivalent of a credit check—no one slipped a fake Rolex past her.

Gorgeous, razor-sharp, and with a BS detector finer than a Savile Row suit, she'd had proposals from men whose trust funds could've bought a small country. But her standards were higher than the Stratosphere viewing platform. Prenup? Blah. She wanted the full *Gilded Age* package.

Lexi hailed from a dynasty of aspirational gold-diggers—though "fools' gold" was more accurate. Her mom had been a stripper downtown back when it was all sticky floors and crumpled dollar bills—hardly gentleman's club glamour. Single mom to Lexi and her two sisters (a collection of Mr. MIA 1989, Mr. Who Cares 1993, and Mr. Who Done It 1997), she'd schooled them in the family trade: Use your god-given assets. And oh, they did.

Her older sister? Still pole-dancing at 34, despite being married to a guy who thought "investment" meant buying a carwash in Henderson. Lexi found it grim; I found it baffling. ("If he's loaded, why's she still grinding?" "Limited mindset, babe.")

The youngest? An OnlyFans entrepreneur and part-time real estate agent. Ran into her once in Whole Foods, pushing a cart of Olipop and protein bars. Shockingly nice. Figure like an Insta model—all filler and filters, but who's judging? Not me, that's who.

Then there was Lexi's mom. Retired now, thanks to a

back stiffer than a White House Secret Service. These days, she "dated" men with social security benefits and a studio apartment downtown.

But Lexi had dodged the family biz like a puddle during flood season. Credit to her face (filler-free, *allegedly*) and a mind sharper than a German tourist glare. She'd realized young that beauty was a debit card, and she'd been swiping it guilt-free ever since.

Lexi's version was high brow—penthouses and Van Cleef without the stiff back.

She smirked, swirling her Stanley cup like it held the secrets of the universe. "He conned the little rat," Lexi continued, eyes glittering with schadenfreude. "Told Heather he wasn't liquid enough—assets tied up in crypto, he'd said— then bounced it with her life savings. No penthouse, no ring, just a bounced check and a broken ego. *Poof.* Vanished quicker than a keg at a frat party."

I arched a brow. "At least it was just a down payment, no?"

She sipped, her mouth curling. "Yeah, a 100K down payment."

I winced. "100K? That's a vacation house in Ohio!"

"First rule of gold-digging is take money, don't give it."

Lexi tapped her temple, smug. "Heather's dumb as a brush. Me? I clocked him as a dud on date two. Still let him pay for everything, though."

"So that's why she came running," I said, wide-eyed. "Trying to recoup her losses?"

"What goes around comes around." She jabbed my arm playfully. "So don't you dare ghost me again, Eva. I'll hex you harder than a witch on a full moon."

"I wasn't ghosting! Do you remember that VIP girl last night? Tegan?"

"The one with the crusty heels?"

"No, not that one. The other one," I blurted, launching into the saga—stolen boyfriends, UFC Dick Print, half a decade of passive-aggressive Instagram posts.

Lexi squinted. "Tegan? The one prancing about in heels taller than her IQ?"

"Same one. Walks around like she's on a cloud, flaunting her Dick Print just to spite me. It's psychological warfare, Lex."

"Hold up—she has a man? For real?" Lexi's brow furrowed, as if Tegan scoring a boyfriend was as likely as a sunny day in Seattle.

"Yes, I've seen them with my own eyes! They go in and

out of the café all the damn time. And I'm *this close*"—I pinched my fingers—"to swiping him. For the principle, of course."

Lexi snorted. "Principle? Babe, you're about as subtle as a stripper at a bachelors. But…" She grinned, shark-like. "If you're gonna chaos-gremlin your way through this, I'm grabbing popcorn."

"Well, I'm gonna. I decided just the other day when he talked my ear off about this and that, UFC stuff. I'd like nothing more than to see Tegan suffer like a—"

"Like you did when she looted your bed? Give it a rest, Eva. That guy's probably off trying to make it as a debt collector, cold calling Boomers out of their life savings."

I huffed. "Maybe, but not this guy. He's the real deal, I think. UFC stuff. Like Connor McGreg or what's his name."

Lexi froze mid-sip, her Stanley cup hovering like she'd just solved *The New York Times* crossword in record speed. "You know what I've just remembered?"

"That you're practically rich and don't know why you even bother clocking in?"

"Everyone's got their hustle, babe. Mine's bagging a man with a trust fund thicker than a Christmas roast. Still clocking in here 'cause—shocker—I actually like getting out of the house and talking to you, and let's face it." She leaned in, lowering her voice as if the motivational posters were eavesdropping. "You're nowhere near a penthouse."

I rolled my eyes. "Oh, please."

"The girl from last night, Tegan, she was grinding on Scott all night. Pretty sure she left with him. Had to thank her for taking one for the team—short-staffed and all that." She smirked a wry little corner-lift. "I know a hustler when I see one. That girl's after a trust fund oldie with the emotional range of a Cup Noodles."

"Ohmygod." My jaw dropped. "She's cheating on Dick Print?" The words fizzed out like a champagne cork. Couldn't even pretend to be upset. A little hiccup that made my life better for once?

"Cheater, hustler, whatever," Lexi shrugged, inspecting her gel nails. "Broke the golden rule, though. Sorry, but she's getting nothing now."

"The 'don't sleep with the mark' rule?"

"Exactly." She sighed, magnanimous as a queen pardoning a jester. "But fine—you're off the hook. At least we got some drama out of your meltdown."

The relief lasted roughly three seconds before Claire—our heavily pregnant receptionist—waddled in, scowling like a Karen mid-rant. "Ladies, we've got a full lobby. Patients aren't here for your nightclub recap, yeah?"

We scattered. Back to the grind: filing charts, soothing hypochondriacs, pretending we hadn't just dissected Tegan's love life with a fine-toothed comb.

But my brain was stuck on loop. Tegan. Scott. Cheating. If she'd gone off with trust fund Scott to bed—the human equivalent of a spreadsheet in a suit—then Eric was getting played harder than a sports bet.

And suddenly, the cosmic scales tipped. Karma hadn't bothered? Fine. I'd be the DIY karma. The kind that shows up with a sledgehammer and a Lowe's receipt.

Lexi's voice slithered into my head. *"Revenge is a dish best served with a side of fries."*

Time to flip the script.

Tegan wanted to play?

Then, let us play.

CHAPTER

NINE

"BITCH, DO I HAVE some piping hot tea for you," I announced as Felicia flopped into my car, her apron speckled with flour and hair reeking of stale espresso.

Her eyes lit up like a Black Friday sale at Ross. "Spill! Finally, you're bringing the drama instead of just moaning about Tegan's Instagram stories."

True. Felicia lived for scandal—especially when it involved Tegan, who'd become our personal villain. After days of my rants about her backstabbing, Felicia was Team Eva all the way. And why wouldn't she be? Tegan had the charm of a parking ticket and the subtlety of a Sunday afternoon honk-fest.

I revved into Lexi's tale, hands flapping like a nutcase. "So, after we left, Lexi had to call in the cavalry. Heather showed up and whisked Ty—the #2 pencil you were slobbering with—off to la-la land. Left poor Scott dateless. And guess who played good samaritan?"

Felicia gasped. "No!"

"Oh, yes. Tegan, being a total 'girl's girl'"—I air-quoted—"talked herself into 'entertaining' Scott. And Tegan, being Tegan, didn't just pour him top-shelf liquor—she poured herself into his lap."

Felicia's jaw dropped. "She cheated on Dick Print with *Scott*? Guy who looks like a hungover mall Santa after a karaoke night?"

I nodded solemnly. "Allegedly."

Felicia slumped back, processing this like a faulty Target self-checkout. "I don't know, Eva. Lexi's about as trustworthy as a politician's promise. And Tegan... I mean, she's a iffy, but cheating? That's a whole other level of messy."

I rolled my eyes. Felicia and Lexi's love/hate relationship was at play—part banter, part showdown. Sometimes, Felicia hated Lexi's everything: her legs (too long), her confidence (too loud), her ability to drain men's wallets faster than a slot machine. Jealous? *Please*. She'd sooner admit to liking cold fries.

"Lexi's never lied to us," I said, a tad too defensive. "And let's face it—Tegan's a walking red flag. Wouldn't trust her to water my neighbors grass."

Felicia folded her arms, skepticism etched like a $20 sale tattoo. "Just saying—Lexi's iffier than a 3 a.m. taco. And Tegan… well, she's Tegan. We don't know her well enough to say."

"I *know* her, Fel!" I snapped, knuckles whitening on the steering wheel. "She's not just a cow—she's a *strategic* cow."

Felicia threw up her hands like I'd flipped off a school zone cross guard. "Alright, keep your Spanx on! I'm just saying—Lexi's probably spiced it up. You know her, she likes her drama well-stirred. Besides, wouldn't Tegan know about the number one rule?"

I exhaled sharply, swerving around a moped with a death wish. "Those are Lexi's rules, not an international billboard on gold digger rules. If Lexi says Tegan rode off into the sunset with Scott's granddad bod, I'm buying it."

Felicia stared out at the sun-soaked highway, silent for once. Then—

"Remember when she lied about her mom being a 'wellness coach'?" She air-quoted, voice dripping with spicy sarcasm. "Turns out 'wellness' meant pole dancing downtown."

I groaned. "Oh, here we go. You cyberstalked her family

like a CIA operative! No one asked you to play two-bit detective in silk pajamas!"

"Please," Felicia scoffed. "Lexi spun a whole *Twilight* backstory till I found her mom's Facebook—'Diamond Delilah,' 5-star reviews on VegasEscortsdotcom. Don't act like that's a Panera resume!"

"It's a job, Fel! Not everyone's mom sells Avon in Henderson! Lexi didn't owe us her life story!"

"Right, because dragging you to date old geezers for free champagne is *totally* normal bestie behavior!" Felicia's voice hit screech level. "The last guy at the club was older than sliced bread! I was saving you from a *Taken* special! For all you knew, she could've been running some madam operation or pulling a Ghislaine Maxwell scheme. I was the only one looking out for you."

"I was an adult!" I barked, nearly hitting a curb. "Knew exactly what I was doing—same as when you—shocker—flirted with Ty's trust fund! If Tegan hadn't crashed it, you'd be Mrs. #2 Pencil by now!"

Felicia flushed tomato-red. "That's a low blow."

I white-knuckled the wheel, counting highway signs to calm down. Felicia's criminology degree made her FBI meets CSI—brilliant, but lethal after two rosés.

It's true—Felicia had a knack for sniffing out secrets like a bloodhound at a CSI wrap party. And yeah, she'd unearthed Lexi's past faster than you could say "Google search history." But here's the kicker: none of us cared that Lexi's mom had once twirled around a pole in the cringiest downtown spot. We were too busy bonding over champagne and girls' night drama and things that actually mattered. If anything, Lexi's backstory made her more interesting. Though, fair play, she still kept Felicia at arm's length—wise move, honestly.

"The point is, Fel," I said, slowing down at the highway exit, "you're fixating on the wrong things."

"So me questioning Lexi's 'credibility'"—she air-quoted like a *Price Is Right* contestant—"is 'wrong' now? Great friend you are."

I scoffed. "Yes, it's wrong," I shot back, voice sharper than a Chili's steak knife. "Lexi literally has zero reason to lie about Tegan! After all the shit I've told you, why are you Team Tegan suddenly? Lexi didn't even know we knew her—to her, Tegan was just some VIP bop with a nice blowout!"

Felicia folded her arms, sulking like a toddler denied a McFlurry. "Lexi spins tales, Eva. Admit it."

I snapped. "Do you tell everyone your mom sobbed into her Burberry scarf when you quit law school to bake raspberry tarts? No? Then stop airing Lexi's dirty laundry like you're on Insta live!"

Her face crumpled. "Low blow, Eva. Even for you."

"Exactly. It stings, yeah? We don't bring up your family meltdowns at girls' night, but you're all 'Ooh, let's dissect Lexi's trauma!' Hypocrite much?"

The car buzzed with tension. I gripped the wheel, knuckles white. I loved Felicia to bits, but her Lexi vendetta was as exhausting as it was misplaced.

"Jesus, I'm just saying Lexi's not Snow White!" Felicia muttered, staring out at the desert landscape apartment parking. "Didn't need to drag my mom into it."

Guilt prickled. "Sorry, Fel. But you're like a dog with a bone when it comes to Lexi. Why would she lie? She didn't even know Tegan existed till last night."

Felicia chewed her lip, voice small. "My parents… you know what they did. It still hurts."

I sighed. We all had skeletons—mine were currently doing a salsa in the trunk. But tonight? We needed a truce. And possibly a Big Gulp rosé.

"I know. Really sorry, Fel," I said, voice softer now that I felt bad about lashing out. "I just want you to hate Tegan like I do, and I guess it's not fair."

Felicia sighed, her anger deflating like a punctured inflatable penis at a bachelorette. "I suppose… maybe you're right about Lexi," she muttered, the words dragging out like a Starbucks line at the mall. Mentioning her parents had been a gut punch—they'd ghosted her harder than a Tinder flake when she ditched law school for baked goods. Now she was stuck riding the bakery on a salary that made In-N-Out look lavish.

"We cool?" I asked, parking outside our apartment, ready to drop this side quest drama.

"Yeah. Still think she's a liar, though."

The drive had felt longer than a Prime ad break, the silence thicker than a double stuffed Oreo. I was tired, starving, and craving a a good shit-talking session about Tegan's latest disaster. Was that really too much to ask?

Just as I caved to agree (fine, maybe Lexi *embellishes*), Felicia blurted, "So if Lexi's not full of it, Tegan's cheating on our boyfriend," she said, taking bell peppers from the fridge like if she were reading my mind. "How sure are we she actually went home with TFB?" *Chop. Chop. Chop.* "Because if I can't trust Lexi to say the truth, I can believe Tegan is a lying sack of potatoes."

"TFB?" I squinted.

"Trust Fund Baby," she clarified, julienning peppers like

a *Chopped* contestant.

I nearly spat out my $6 rosé. "You mean TFMAM."

"The *what* now?"

"Trust Fund *Middle-Aged Man*."

We cackled like hyenas, saying other misnomers ("How about TFMAMB?" "What's that?" "Trust Fund Middle-Aged Man Boobs!" har, har, har), the earlier fight forgotten. Soon, we were roasting Tegan's poor taste in cheating partners louder than a bar on fight night.

"So what'd she actually do with Scott, anyway?" Felicia asked, leaning in like a shameless gossip.

"Dunno," I said, paprika snowing over the chicken. "Lexi got cut off by Claire before she could say. But I'll grill her about it tomorrow."

"You'll text me the deets, yeah?"

"Of course!" I hissed, sizzling chicken like my life depended on it. "Every grim, geriatric detail."

Felicia pulled a face. "She's quite nasty, that one, huh? Guess she didn't learn the golden rules to successful gold-digging."

I squinted. "I guess neither did we. Didn't get that Ono, and trust me, I'm still thinking about it."

"Me too! Ten bands down Lexi's throat like that"—she snapped her fingers—"gone."

We cackled a bit more at Lexi's escapades, and even laughed at our own selves, trying and failing at the whole gold-digging thing like a bad investment, but guilt eventually nipped at me. Felicia could roast Lexi until their feud resumed, so I threw in the towel before she got too creative. Honestly, shit-talking Tegan was far more therapeutic—like a Groupon spa day for the soul.

"You're right, E," Felicia sighed, slopping guac onto a tortilla. "Can't stay angry forever. Plus, if I stay mad at you, I'll have to move out, and let's face it—we can't afford to live alone."

"Or you'll have to go back to law school and appease your parents for rent money."

Felicia made a face. "Oh, shut your mouth."

We snorted, the last of our silly fight dissolving like cotton candy in water. Just as I was assembling a fajita that could've won *Chopped*, my phone buzzed. Cali.

"Jason's having boys' night tomorrow—code for beer and nachos, of course—so we're doing girls' night," she announced, no hello. "Mom's got Rubi. Bring Lexi and the rest. I'm quite ready for a good time."

I turned to Felicia, my eyes lighting up. "Girls' night tomorrow!"

Next evening, I pulled up to Cali's an hour early—not by choice, but because she'd threatened to revoke my auntie privileges with Rubi if I didn't "help style the charcuterie." (Translation: fluff outdoor cushions like a Ralph Lauren ad and arrange the charcuterie board with more cheeses than I could name.)

"Tablecloth needs ironing. Or at least a smooth-over," Cali barked, thrusting a stack of plates at me. "And the olives go kitty-corner to the crackers, Eva. Come on."

"Remember when we snuck out to parties with kegs and underage drinking?" I said, nostalgia hitting like a delayed school bus.

"The gold ol' days," Cali sighed, but her orders didn't stop.

"The ham here?" I asked pointing at the only empty spot.

"*Prosciutto*, not ham." She took over, moving me out of the way. "Right here, see?" Pointing to the exact spot I'd asked about.

"Now we're nearly thirty, drink wine instead of beer, yet here we are."

"Think we'll have a nice time or some fight or other will break out? Hate when that happens."

"Speak for yourself. I'm here for the TFMAM tea."

"The *what*?"

"You'll see," I grinned, buzzing like a Pop-Tart timer.

The doorbell chimed. We froze, mid-margarita pour.

"Okay," Cali said, smoothing her Zara jumpsuit. "Let's get this show on the road."

Game on.

CHAPTER

TEN

"THIS MARG'S BANGING," Felicia declared, sloshing her third glass onto Cali's outdoor rug. Our "signature blend" was basically Lee's Discount finest tequila, a splat of grenadine (for the 'gram), and jalapeño slices for a kick. Cali and Felicia had invented it during a *Love Island* finale meltdown, and now it was our go-to for any emotional crisis—breakups, *Bridgerton*, *Bake Off* eliminations.

We were crammed around Cali's Pottery Barn fire pit—a "rustic-chic" number she loved more than me, probably. She'd banged on about it for weeks after her *Homes & Gardens* phase while she was nesting with Rubi, or so she'd said. The pool glowed like an XS disco ball, and the "meticulously landscaped" garden (i.e.: a few succulents and a Lowe's water feature) almost made you forget we were in Vegas. Desert chill? Bah. Between the fire and the Costco fleece blankets, we were toasty.

"That's because I doubled the tequila," Lexi slurred, swaying like a regular at her mom's old club (*oopsie*).

It was very lush, this—Cali sipping her virgin piña colada (on account of the breastfeeding, she said), very pregnant Claire nibbling smoked something-or-other cheese, and the rest of us three sheets to the wind. The kind of night where you laugh till your Spanx roll down.

This, I thought, *is why we endure Tinder fails and Desert Blooms loyalty schemes.*

Then Lexi, ever the provocateur wannabe, leaned in, eyes glittering like a chandelier. "Okay, ladies. Truth time. Have any of you ever had public sex?"

"Does a Fiat 500 count?" I asked, grinning.

Felicia snorted marg out her nose. "Obviously!"

"What about… airplane bathroom?" Claire deadpanned, nibbling a carrot stick like she'd asked about the weather.

"That's the mile-high club, babe," Felicia wheezed, wiping tears with a Chipotle napkin from her purse.

"Overrated," Lexi drawled, launching into a graphic review of American Airline bathrooms that left us howling like hyenas.

Cali's laughter bubbled over like a champagne fountain at a bachelorette, and I couldn't help but grin. My sister's optimism was the kind that could power a small village—or at least survive a trash TV finale without cynicism. Annoying? Occasionally. Endearing? Always.

"So, Cali," I said, flopping onto the sofa like a deflated blow-up doll, "Felicia and I attempted to 'network' with trust fund babies last weekend. Except, it turns out they were more trust fund middle-aged men."

Lexi snorted into her drink. "They're not middle aged! More like experienced philanthropists—"

"Fine! Not middle-aged men, then. A little over," I cut in. "Okay, okay philanthropists with granddad bods and a *Times* crossword addiction," I said, a bout of laughter threatening to escape. "Felicia dubbed them TFMAMs. Trust Fund Middle-Aged Men™."

The room erupted. Even Lexi, who'd spent the week defending Charles' "distinguished silver fox energy," nearly spilled her drink.

"But they're so rich," Lexi protested, swatting my arm. "Charles alone owns a vineyard in France!"

"A vineyard he can't pronounce," Felicia muttered.

Lexi launched into her retelling of the night, spinning it into a *Love Is Blind* meets *Millionaire Matchmaker* saga. When she hit the Tegan plot twist, Felicia choked on her cracker, eyes watering.

"Hold up," Cali interrupted, her virgin-drink-focus sharpening. "Tegan? High school friend turned boyfriend staler? That Tegan?"

"The very one," I sighed, bracing for Cali's trademark "karma cuddle" speech. My sister believed in universal justice like it was a Uber Eats service—order righteousness, receive promptly. But karma was slower than snail mail these days, and I'd decided to play mail lady.

"Ugh, she's awful," Cali said. "But don't stoop to her level, Eva. Rise above! Be the bigger person!"

The bigger person was currently plotting to "accidentally" steal Tegan's man.

"It gets worse," I groaned, diving into the Tesla snub. Then, because I couldn't *not* talk about him, I said, "Eric— her current boyfriend—has a prominent... *ahem*... sweats situation."

Felicia snorted. "Dick print. Just say it. We call him Dick Print, for Pete's sake."

"Felicia!" Cali gasped, clutching her sweater like a stress ball.

"It's nice to look at, I admit." We shared a laugh at Eric's dick print expense. "And then," I barreled on, "Tegan was caught canoodling with Scott—the same TFMAM I went on that 'networking' night out with Lexi. All this, mind, with a boyfriend likely sitting at home eating protein chips and wondering where his girlfriend is."

"Still the same old Tegan, then," Cali muttered.

"Dunno how anyone cheats, honestly," Felicia chimed in, nibbling a piece of cheese. "If you're not up for commitment, just be a grownup and be done with it."

Lexi, who'd been quieter than a library during finals, finally piped up. "Look, I didn't even know you guys knew her. She was just... nice. Too nice, if you catch my drift. When you're with a man who's flashing cash like he's in a *Casino Royale* remake, the girls swarm like seagulls on bread crumbs. So, no, it wasn't weird she jumped on Scott. I'd have handled it myself, but she volunteered. Probably, she went full *Striptease* on him—did stuff I wouldn't touch with a vaulting pole. Bet he tipped her enough for a week in the Maldives, though."

"So she's, what—a trash gold digger?" Felicia asked, side-eyeing me. "Because Eva went on and on about not going home with the target, and if she doesn't know the number one rule, then what does she know, am I right?"

"Exactly," Lexi said, nodding like a bobblehead now that she had a little liquor in her. "She's all eagerness, zero finesse. Even you've got more game, Fel, and you know nothing about nothing."

The room erupted into *Housewives*-level chatter. Lexi wasn't just saying Tegan shacked up with some random millionaire—she was implying she'd gone full *Fifty Shades* at the freaking Wynn. Wild, even by Lexi's standards. I bit my tongue, though part of me was dying to ask: *Did they use the mini-bar? I hear those things can get pricey, but then again, a weekend at the Maldives…*

Claire, our sweet-as-pie and very pregnant coworker, finally blurted the question we'd all dodged, "Sorry, but… what do you actually do for these guys? Why were you babysitting Scott?"

Lexi smirked, swirling her drink. "Entertaining, peach. Keep 'em happy, keep 'em spending. Think of me as a… luxury concierge with better eyeliner."

Felicia choked on her guac chip. "Luxury *what*? You drank our Onos, and they're ten bands each!"

Lexi shrugged. "You left them! Waste not, want not!"

Cali wasn't as peachy as the rest of us, saying, "But what do you actually do for the men? It sounds all sorts of bad. Like a bad twist on *Indecent Proposal*."

Lexi's eyes narrowed, her manicured grip tightening on

her bottom shelf liquor marg. "I don't *do* anything for them except enjoy their company—and fine, their Amex Black. Couldn't give a rat's ass what you guys think, so save the lecture," she snipped, her voice sharper than a tack. Never mind that Cali's raised brow was the only hint of judgment—Lexi's armor was permanently welded on, polished by years of Vegas nightclub side-eye.

She paused, sipping her drink with the poise of a high-priced escort, then waved a hand dismissively. "That night, I told the men I'd bring two friends—Eva and Felicia—but they vanished faster than a keg at a frat party. I felt a smidge responsible, so I fixed it. Standard girlfriend activities."

The group exchanged glances. Lexi's version of "fixing it" could range from booking an Uber to brokering a peace treaty.

Cali, ever the poster child for middle-class morals, wrinkled her nose like she'd stepped in a puddle outside Sprouts. "But why is it your job to play Cupid? Sounds a bit... Tinder-for-hire. And roping Eva and Felicia into it? Not cool."

Lexi's jaw clenched, her lips twitching into a sneer. "Okay. Let's spell this out so you simpletons can understand," she hissed, her Sambas tapping the patio tiles like a frustrated metronome. "I'm not running a damn

Introduction Agency for millionaires from my iPhone. Charles—" she dropped the name like a Gucci clutch on a Chili's table, "—is my *boyfriend*. Meet-the-friends-at-the-Wynn boyfriend. Older? Sure. Rich? Obviously. But he's not some sugar daddy funding my Chanel habit. We do weekends at the Malibu beach house, not 'arrangements' in Motel 6. Got it?"

Cali opened her mouth, then wisely opted to nibble a guac-dipped carrot stick instead.

"I'm dating a man whose trust fund could buy your entire zip code," Lexi continued, flicking her hair with the drama of a corner prostitute with a bad attitude. "Doesn't make me a working girl. Makes me strategic and fucking smart. And if I want to set my girls up with his rich banker friends, that's called social climbing, babe. Not a crime."

Cali just stared.

"Before you start diagnosing my life choices," Lexi snapped, her voice as sharp as her contour, "Know that Charles adores me. He treats me like a queen. Which, FYI, includes funding my living and shopping habits. So yes, he's in his 'masculine energy'—" she air-quoted, rolling her eyes so hard I feared for her eyelash extensions, "—and I'm in my 'princess era.' Got it?"

We nodded in unison, the way one might placate a

disgruntled goose.

Lexi smoothed her top and continued. "Charles has friends. Single, loaded friends who enjoy spoiling women who aren't their ex-wives. So I thought, *Why not play Cupid?* Eva and Felicia are single, gorgeous, and infinitely less dull than Heather's yoga retreat stories." She shot me a look. "But *someone* decided to ghost faster than a Tinder swipe after a 'Should we split the bill?' conversation."

I sank lower into the sofa, mentally drafting my application to Witness Protection.

"So I called Heather," Lexi said. "And then Tegan swooped in, batting her lashes at Scott like a pro. But honestly?" She tossed her hair, a move perfected by years of watching *Housewives*. "I was doing charity work. That's it, that's the whole of it."

The room pulsed with thick tension. Cali, ever the peacemaker, opened her mouth again—but Lexi wasn't done.

"And for the record," she added, jabbing a glittery nail at us, "I'm not a gold digger. I'm a luxury experience curator. Charles gets arm candy; I get Louboutins. Everyone wins."

I bit my lip to stop from laughing. Only Lexi could spin "dating rich men" into a LinkedIn-worthy career.

Cali, said, "But Eva said Scott's breath smelled like—"

"Irrelevant," Lexi cut in, waving a dismissive hand. "The point is, I'm a strategist. And if you guys can't see that, maybe you're just jealous my love language is 'bank transfer' and yours is stuck somewhere between 'should I go halfsies or is it my turn to pay the whole bill.'"

Felicia snorted into her glass. "Mine's 'free snacks,' so..."

The tension dissolved like sugar in a Mojito. Lexi's phone buzzed—a text from Charles, no doubt, and she flounced out, leaving a cloud of vanilla-scented defiance in her wake.

"Well," Cali said, breaking the silence, "she's... passionate."

"Passionate? She's a one-woman *Ocean's 11*," I muttered.

But secretly, I admired her. Lexi didn't just play the game —she wrote the rulebook, laminated it, and sold it on Etsy.

Lexi came back with a smile on her face, probably from a big tip, no doubt nothing close to a weekend at Maldives, but something close to it.

"So there were no expectations for Eva and Felicia?" Cali pressed, her voice tinged with that newfound mom concern she'd perfected since joining the Babycenter group.

Lexi rolled her eyes, her acrylic nail tapping against her glass cup like a judge's gavel. "Is there anything else you can talk about? Perhaps Rubi's first throw up or how she projectile pooped in your eye. Something, *anything* else, please."

Cali sighed, shoulders dropping like a deflated Valentine's Day balloon. "Alright, alright. Not judging, Lex. I just worry about Eva, is all."

Lexi's glare softened, the fire dimming to a hint of understanding. "Chill, yeah? I'd never throw Eva—or any of you—into the deep end without a life jacket. Scout's honor."

The vibe shifted heavier than an unwanted DJ mix at XS. Lexi's dating history—*rich, richer, richest*—clashed with Claire's Happily Married Since 2016 and Cali's Dentist & Great Dad bliss. Claire, glowing like a Clearblue pregnancy test ad, was oceans away from Lexi's gold digger antics. And Cali had married her college sweetheart, a guy who thought date night meant a Domino's and *Die Hard* followed by *Love Actually* just to make Cali happy. Different universes, same group chat.

Needing to puncture the tension, I blurted, "Fel had a on-nighter with a Tinder swipe last year and had to book it to CVS for the morning-after pill!" I exhaled, feeling lighter already. "God, that felt good to say."

Felicia's margarita went airborne. "You cow! That was ages ago!" she screeched, face redder than Taco Bell's Extra

Hot sauce.

I cackled, half-drunk on tequila and schadenfreude. The group erupted—Claire nearly dropped her drink, Cali snorted into her cashmere dupe.

"Your face!" Lexi wheezed, dabbing her eyes with one of Felicia's Chipotle napkins. "Worth the blackmail alone!"

And just like that, the mood lifted like a Spirit flight to Sedona. We traded cringe stories, Cali's Hinge date who'd brought his mom (two before she met Jason, of course), Lexi's Raya disaster with a guy who collected My Little Pony and been a child star, Claire's "I tripped into a bush on my first kiss" saga. My "I dated my Peloton instructor and had to quit when I bolted" drama.

Embarrassing? Obviously. But that's the magic of girls' night—turning mortification into laughs, one Trader Joe's cheeseboard at a time.

CHAPTER

ELEVEN

⟡

THE NEXT SATURDAY MORNING, Desert Bloom Café was its usual oasis of chaos—a symphony of clattering cups, Felicia muttering curses at the espresso machine, and the scent of pastry lingering. I was wedged in my favorite corner table, pretending to read *Bridget Jones* for the 47th time, when he walked in.

Eric.

Tegan's Eric.

My future Eric, if Operation Steal-a-Boyfriend (draft title) went according to plan—a plan currently scribbled on a napkin and involved "accidentally" spilling latte art on his shirt. Thing was, I had no idea how to actually do it. I'd just thought about it. *Wing it*, I thought. *How hard could it be?*

My stomach did a somersault usually reserved for tequila shots and tax audits. *Stay cool, Eva. Channel Lexi. Or at least someone who's watched a Bond film.*

But let's be real—my seduction skills peaked and died ages ago, so I was really going into this blind. Mind, it wasn't a Tinder swipe, either. It was Dick-Print-Eric, and he had me sweating from all sorts of orifices.

"Hey, Eva." Eric grinned, sliding into the table like he'd been invited. His presence was unfairly calming, like a human Xanax in a gym hoodie, that same clean scent clinging to him.

"Hi, Eric!" I chirped, voice two octaves too high. *Fucking smooth.*

He nodded at my book. "*Bridget Jones*, huh?"

"Research," I blurted. "For a friend. Who's writing a thesis. On… singleton tropes."

Kill me now.

He actually laughed, sounding like a train at midnight. "What's it now, another baby?"

I gave him a look that said, *you read this?*

"My sister reads it, and since we have nothing else to really talk about, she tells me all about her books."

"Ah," I said, and smiled, closing my book since he looked ready to stay.

Felicia materialized, slamming down a cortado with a

smirk. "Here's your research beverage, Shakespeare."

Eric laughed—a warm, crinkly-eyed sound that made my traitorous heart flutter. *Focus, Eva.* This was, after all, war territory. A war with very nice forearms.

"So," he said, leaning in, "you come here often?"

I choked on my cortado. *Was he… flirting?*

"Only when Felicia's experimenting with those tarts," I said, pointing to my slice.

He chuckled, and suddenly, the plan didn't matter. The nerves melted like a Magnum in the sun, replaced by something dangerously close to giddiness.

"Wanna split a cinnamon bun?" he asked, nodding at the display case. "They're half-off if you pretend it's breakfast."

"Is it still breakfast at noon?"

"In Spain, sure."

I flipped my hair back and turned on my version of siren eyes. "Alright, then," I whispered, channeling my inner siren like Lexi did.

His eyes lingered on me. I swear I melted. "What can I say? Felicia's cinnamon buns are better than my protein pancakes."

I smirked, then—*god help me*—bit my lip. Just a nibble.

His gaze snapped to my mouth, captivated. *Score.* I leaned back, feeling like Vivian Ward in *Pretty Woman*.

It's just payback, it's just payback, I thought, my guilty conscience already catching up to me like a good lapsed catholic.

If Tegan could see me now, she'd throw me into Lake Mead in a blue barrel.

We talked a bit more before he sauntered off to order, but those two minutes left my brain doing somersaults. Shit. I'd memorized his order—cappuccino, extra foam, and today, a cinnamon bun to share—like some pathetic rom-com lead. I buried my nose in my book, but my mind was already drafting a *Notting Hill*-meets-*Fifty Shades* fanfic. Picnics in Town Square! Smooching in a black cab! Him shirtless, doing the dishes in my IKEA furnished apartment!

Jesus, was I *this* desperate?

It's just payback, it's just payback.

Then again, with Tegan off necking randos at the Wynn, why shouldn't I flirt with her leftovers? Revenge was a dish best served with a side of guilt-free eye candy.

And if eye candy was the order of the day, I'd say martial arts clearly did a man good—his ass looked like it had been sculpted by a Greek sculptor. I wondered if he had any UFC fights on stream. Probably on some niche ESPN channel. Not that I'd watch. I'd faint quicker than a PT's Pub pint at last orders if I saw blood.

...Unless he's the one doling out the punches.

After ordering, he ambled back to my table like he owned the place, plonking himself beside me as if we were two regulars attached at the hip. Meanwhile, my brain was doing a salsa routine between *This is working! Amazing!* and *You're a disaster, Eva Torres, and mom would agree*. Not only was he finer than a quarterback at Super Bowl, he was also *Tegan's* Dick Print. Terrifying. Deliciously terrifying.

But Jesus—those dimples? That stubble? It was like the universe had designed him specifically to test my moral compass. Which, let's be honest, was currently pointing firmly toward petty revenge.

Focus, Eva. He's a means to an end. A six-foot, biceps-for-days end.

"How'd Pilates go this morning?" he asked, giving me half a cinnamon bun. Too bad it hadn't been one plate, one fork.

"Fine. Just… bending. Pretending to be a pretzel," I said, cringing. How had I somehow memorized his routine? Was I playing chess or checkers here? But then, how did he know I'd just stepped out of the reformer and into the café? Jury was out.

He grinned—little flirt—and leaned in. "You should try jiu-jitsu. I think you'd like it."

"Not really my vibe," I said, though the mental image of us tangled on a mat (*Oops, slipped!*) nearly short-circuited my brain. Tegan would spontaneously combust. I bit back a smirk.

"Come on, it's all controlled," he said, voice smooth and low. "Trust me—I'm a professional." *Wink.*

I melted.

If I didn't know better, I'd swear he was flirting. Which, let's face it, only made me channel my inner *Bridget Jones: Hello, Mr. Darcy, let's frolic in a fountain.*

No. Bad Eva. He's a revenge plot, not a life plan.

But then he shifted, his arm brushing mine, and I thought, *Screw it. If Tegan can steal boyfriends, so can I.*

I was mid-sentence, "Maybe I'll give it a go, if you promise not to snap me like a twig," when the café door swung open. And there she was. Tegan.

My smile dropped faster than you can say home wrecker while Eric said, "Of course not. I'll go extra easy on you." But I wasn't paying attention because the room didn't just go cold —it went full *Game of Thrones* in winter time. Tegan's

Stepford-wife grin vanished the second she saw Eric beside me, her icy blue eyes narrowing.

Her energy shifted, dark and crackling like a storm cloud over the Caesars beer garden. And weirdly, I loved it. Even as my stomach did a nasty flip, I felt a thrill.

"Hey, babe," she cooed, planting a kiss on Eric's cheek like she was marking her territory with her presence. "Eva. What a surprise."

"Likewise," I said, my voice steadier than my knees. For once, I didn't shrink into the wallpaper. Part of me wanted to scream, *I know about Scott, you backstabbing witch!* And just lay it all out, but the sensible bit—the one that remembered I was in public—kept me in check.

Also, I was scared.

Tegan laughed—a sound as genuine as a Ross Rolex. "Eric, honey, Brody needs you back at the gym."

Eric, blissfully unaware of the war unfolding over his cappuccino and half cinnamon bun, nodded and stood. "Bye, Eva. See you around."

As he left, Tegan's gaze stayed locked on me, sharp as a stiletto. I'd seen that look before—right before she swiped my man and my job. But this time, I didn't flinch.

"What do you think you're playing at, Eva?" she hissed,

her voice low and venomous. "Eric's *mine*. Don't forget that."

"If he's yours," I shot back, chin up, "you've got nothing to worry about."

For a split second, I felt like Bridget Jones in a rom-com montage, the one where everything goes wrong until it finally goes right. Then reality hit. Tegan wasn't just a villain—she was a goddamn liability.

Jesus. What have I done?

Tegan's smirk sharpened into something venomous, like a designer stiletto poised to stomp on a dollar bin sandal. "Oh, darling," she purred, flicking her glossy platinum hair over one shoulder. "Do you really think you're competition? Look at you. *Look at me*. Who's holding the Amex and who's covered in coffee stains in dupe Lululemon?"

She'd always been the human equivalent of a *Check Engine* light in my life—blinking smugly through every triumph, from nabbing my lifeguard gig to parading her Tesla through a snowstorm like she was hosting Formula 1. But this time, I had receipts.

"Eric's *mine*," she hissed, leaning in so close I caught a whiff of her $500-per-bottle "I'm Better Than You" perfume. "Back. Off."

I channeled my inner Lexi and grinned. "Which one, though? Eric... or Scott?"

The name hung in the air two seconds too long. Tegan's spray-tanned complexion faded to the color of twice ran coffee. "How—"

"Oh, please," I interrupted, waving a hand like I was swatting a wasp. "I know all about you and Scott. Although, I suppose calling it a relationship might be a stretch, don't you think?" I pressed my hand to my mouth, feigning a laugh. "Couldn't even drag it out like a proper gold digger."

Tegan's composure crumbled. With a guttural noise usually reserved for spin class, she hoisted the café table— sending my cortado airborne—and slammed it hard enough flip, the table landing against the wall. The half-eaten cinnamon bun somersaulted tragically to the floor.

The room froze. A toddler in the corner clapped.

I was up now, the table turned over in the corner, but I didn't back down. "Or what?" I pressed, adrenaline surging like I'd mainlined a Red Bull. "What are you going to do that you haven't already done?" It was a moment of bravery, I'll say that.

Tegan's eyes darted around the café, where six phones were now discreetly recording. Her horror was palpable—a woman who'd rather be caught dead than viral in last season's Zara.

Felicia, who'd been aggressively frothing milk, vaulted the counter wielding a tray like a weapon. "Tegan! Out! Now! Before I 'accidentally' pour oat milk on your vintage Gucci!"

"This isn't over," she spat, storming out so violently the doorbell jingled a cheerful *Good riddance!*

I slumped into a chair, my hands trembling like a soufflé in a earthquake. "Did I just… win?"

Felicia tossed me a look. "You Britney-Spears-circa-2007'd her. That was iconic."

Iconic or stupid, I thought.

"What the actual hell just happened?" Felicia whispered, clutching the tray like a shield. The café was silent, save for the faint hum of the espresso machine and the sound of a toddler loudly asking, "Mommy, why did that lady throw the table?"

"I think… I just became the drama."

Felicia raised an eyebrow. "And how does it feel?"

"Not as fun as being on the other side."

Tegan's meltdown had been more explosive than an egg in a microwave. One mention of Scott, and she'd gone full

Housewives—table-flipping, fake tan fading, and all. The memory of her face, pale beneath the orange glow, sent a shiver down my spine.

"All I did was say I knew about Scott," I said, still processing. "And she went full *Exorcist*."

Felicia snorted. "Guess Lexi wasn't exaggerating, then. Tegan's probably terrified Eric will find out."

"But why?" I frowned. "Even if I told him, why would he believe me over her? She's his girlfriend. I'm just a random girl at a café."

Felicia leaned in, lowering her voice. "Unless… there's already trouble in paradise. Maybe Eric's not as clueless as she thinks."

The thought hit me like a rogue teabag to the face. Tegan's fear wasn't just about keeping up appearances—it was real. The kind of real that comes with late-night arguments, unanswered texts, and the sinking feeling that your house of cards is one gust of wind away from collapse.

"She's scared," I said slowly. "But of what? Scott? Eric? Or… both?"

Felicia's eyes widened. "What if Scott's not just a fling? What if he's her Plan B?"

"Or her Plan A," I countered. "What if Eric's already

suspicious, and she's trying to keep the plates spinning before they all come crashing down?"

"Tegan's finally made a mistake."

"And her empire's built on quicksand," I added, a strange mix of satisfaction and dread bubbling in my chest.

As the café slowly returned to normal—Shane mopping up spilled cortado, customers pretending they hadn't just witnessed a meltdown worthy of *Housewives*—I realized Tegan's downfall wasn't just about me. It was about *her*. Her lies, her secrets, her desperate need to stay on top.

And for the first time, I felt a flicker of pity.

Then Felicia handed me a tart. "Eat this. You've earned it."

I took a bite, the crust melting on my tongue. "You think she'll come back?"

"Oh, she'll be back," Felicia said. "But next time, we'll be ready."

I nodded, the adrenaline fading into something steadier. Tegan's house of cards was wobbling, and I wasn't sure if I wanted to watch it fall… or help it come down.

Either way, the game had changed.

CHAPTER

TWELVE

❧

"SCOTT'S DEAD," LEXI ANNOUNCED, leaning against the doorframe like she was auditioning for *Grey's Anatomy*.

The needle box slipped from my hand, splattering needles across the floor like a Rorschach test of panic. "Scott's dead?" I gasped, my mind racing to the worst possible conclusion—Tegan, armed with a Gucci handbag and a grudge, had silenced the only man who knew her secrets.

Lexi burst into laughter, doubling over like I'd just told her UMC wait times were down to five minutes. "No, you walnut! Scott's *deaf*! He got a hearing aid!"

I blinked, my heart still thudding like a metronome on *presto*. "You said dead."

"I said deaf! Honestly, Eva, your ears are worse than his were." She sashayed into the room, her heeled Crocs clicking like a countdown to chaos. "Anyway, this is huge. You know what this means, right?"

I stared at her, picking up stray needles off the floor. "That… he can finally hear Charles' golf stories?"

Lexi groaned, tossing her extensions to the side. "No, you dope. It means Charles is next! They're practically twins— same age, same hobbies, same obsession with 'vintage' Rolexes. It's only a matter of time before he's got a hearing aid, too."

I paused, mid-sweep. "And this is… bad?"

"Bad?" Lexi gasped, clutching her chest like I'd suggested she downgrade to non-heeled Crocs. "It's a crisis! Do you know how hard it is to flirt with a man who keeps saying 'What?' every five seconds? It's like dating a confused parrot."

I stifled a laugh. "Maybe he'll just lip-read?"

"Lip-read?" Lexi repeated, horrified. "Do you know how much Botox I've invested in these lips? They're not moving for anyone."

As she launched into a tirade about the "inconvenience" of aging men, I couldn't help but smile. Lexi's world was a whirlwind of champagne problems and designer dilemmas, and somehow, it was exactly the distraction I needed from

Tegan's looming drama.

Still, as I collected needles, I couldn't shake the image of Scott—alive, thankfully—with his shiny new hearing aid. If Tegan's empire was built on secrets, how long before someone *heard* the truth?

"I just don't date men who remember the moon landing, alright? So, no, I don't know jack about hearing aids or Botoxed lips, for that matter."

"Jesus, someone woke up on the wrong side of bed," Lexi said, pouting like an escort on the prowl. Her usual sparkle dimmed, and guilt hit me at once.

I might not get her thing for silver foxes, but I got her. Dating someone who thinks *The Beatles* are still cutting-edge must come with its own set of headaches. Different playlists and everything.

The few times I'd tagged along to Lexi's trust fund soirées, I'd felt like a Trader Joe's premade at an on Strip tea party. But Lexi? She shone. Young, gorgeous, and with the confidence of someone who knows how to work a room— and a wallet.

"Okay," I said, nudging her. "Let's grab lunch. You can tell me all about Scott and his shiny new hearing aid."

An hour-long lunch break at the local Olive Garden was hardly the Ritz, but it was just enough time to inhale a pasta and dissect the latest office gossip without resorting to interpretive dance to explain why Dr. Perez definitely dyes his beard. Plus, the restaurant staff practically treated us like heroes, all because we rolled up in scrubs like we'd just sprinted out of a *Grey's Anatomy* episode. Never mind that our clinic was a glorified walk-in hut next to an H&R Block. Perks were perks, even if they came with a side of mistaken identity.

"I'd sell my soul for a mimosa," Claire announced, glaring at her sparkling water. Pregnancy had turned our once-reserved friend into a hybrid of Shakespearean tragedian and unhinged TikTok comments. Last week, she'd described her baby's kicks as "*Dancing With The Stars* auditions in my ribs," and honestly, we were all living for it.

"Babe, after you evict that baby, we'll toast with entire bottles," Lexi said, inspecting a menu for carb counts. "But for now, stick to juice. We can't have the staff thinking we're *that* kind of medical professionals. Just enjoy it, it won't last." She shot a suspicious look at a waiter refilling breadsticks, as if he might report us to *The Las Vegas Sun* for frivolous brunching.

Claire sighed. "If one more person tells me to 'enjoy the peace before the chaos,' I'm going to fake a contraction in their handbag."

We dissolved into laughter, the kind that drew side-eye from a table of retirees nibbling garlic bread. For a moment, life felt blissfully simple—no worries, no Tegan, just friends and overpriced strawberry lemonade.

Then Claire threw a grenade. "So. Tegan. What's the latest? Did she finally get dumped for cheating?"

The table fell silent. A breadstick snapped in Lexi's grip.

"Where to even begin," I said, launching into the saga of Tegan's café meltdown—the table-flipping, the threats, the way she'd stormed out like a disgraced politician. "And now every time Eric smiles at me, I'm half-convinced she's lurking in a bush with a taser."

Lexi gasped. "Eric? The UFC wannabe? You're holding out on us!"

"It's not like that!" I protested, though my traitorous face flared redder than Lexi post-Botox flush. "I'm just strategically avoiding emotional entanglements. And possible felony charges."

Claire leaned in, eyes sparkling. "Please, you're not

avoiding feelings. You're feeling out an undertake."

Lexi nodded sagely. "And Eric's the taking?"

"Or the under," Claire said. "Eva's the take."

"That metaphor's gone rogue," I muttered, stealing a fry off her plate.

But they weren't wrong. Tegan was everywhere, like a chat group you couldn't leave, and Eric… well, Eric was the human equivalent of a Christmas latte—sweet, addictive, and guaranteed to ruin my sleep schedule.

"Just promise me one thing," Claire said, pointing her straw at me like a scepter. "If you do take him, send Tegan a selfie. For research purposes."

"Claire!"

"What? The baby wants drama!"

Honestly, picking up Felicia from the café felt like prepping for a zombie showdown. Tegan's last meltdown had been about as subtle as a sequin overdose, and if she clocked my plans to swipe her UFC Dick Print? Welp. Let's just say I'd need Lexi's Botox connect for reconstruction.

But here's the kicker: her rage only fueled my resolve. Flirting with Eric wasn't just petty—it was art. And watching Tegan unravel? Worth every flutter of my anxiety-riddled heart. Sure, someone might get hurt but statistically, probably not me. (*Famous last words, Eva.*)

"Tegan's a nut," Lexi announced, sipping her strawberry lemonade. "Went full *Fifty Shades* on Scott, and she barely knew the man. Not exactly target etiquette, is it?" She shot Claire a wink. "Sugar daddy target."

Claire—perched on the edge of her Olive Garden chair like it might combust—rolled her eyes. "Yes, Lexi. I've gathered."

Lexi shrugged, unfazed. "Not my circus, not my clowns. Girl's got audacity, I'll give her that." She smirked, leaning in. "Let's just say she's more Motel 6 than the Four Seasons. Pretty soon Scott's friends will be calling her a sure thing, what with all the stuff she did to him."

"What stuff?" Claire asked, cheeks pinker than a *Barbie* promo. Pregnancy had turned her into a libertine—or maybe it was Lexi's habit of oversharing between bites of pasta.

"Oh, spill!" I chimed in, leaning so far forward I nearly face-planted the Alfredo sauce. Knowledge was power, and Tegan's dirty laundry was like holding a nuclear button. After years of her *Housewives*-level dramatics, I was ready to weaponize every sordid detail.

Lexi's grin turned feral. "Let's just say it involves travel-sized lube and a TripAdvisor review of his penthouse headboard."

"What does that mean?" Claire and I said in tandem.

I mentally filed it under Revenge Excel Sheet Tab 3: Nuclear Options.

"Alright, alright!" Lexi announced, leaning in with the gravitas of a White House correspondent breaking news about a scandalous affair. "Charles spilled the tea last night—though, fair warning, it's more *Golden Bachelor* than *Bachelor*. Apparently, Tegan's into…" She paused, her Angelina Jolie lips quirking. "…erotic asphyxiation. You know. Choking. For funsies."

Claire choked on her sparkling water. "*Choking?* Like 'Help, I've swallowed a Costco hot dog whole' choking?!"

"No, you dunce," Lexi sighed, as if explaining TikTok to a Victorian ghost. "*Erotic* choking. You let someone cut off your airflow during… *you know*… to make the big O hit harder. Think of it like adding chili flakes to your avocado toast. Spicy. Dangerous. Potentially regrettable."

I blinked, suddenly questioning my entire existence. Here I was, proud of remembering to exfoliate weekly, while Tegan was out here treating intimacy like an extreme sport. "So it's like *Fifty Shades of Senior Citizen*?"

"Exactly!" Lexi jabbed a manicured finger at me. "But

here's the kicker—she did it with some rich guy she'd just met at a VIP. Two hours prior! No safe word, no background check, nothing. Charles said the man's idea of aftercare was sending her home in an Uber."

Claire's eyes widened, her hand drifting protectively to her bump. "That's not *spicy*, that's *call a lawyer*!"

"Tell me about it," Lexi said, biting a breadstick. "You'd have better luck trusting an IKEA instruction manual. One wrong move and—*poof*—you're a *Dateline* episode."

I grimaced, visions of Tegan and Scott playing *Hunger Games: Couples Edition* flashing in my mind. "So she's basically fast-dating Darwinism?"

"Yes!" Lexi cried, as if I'd finally grasped quantum physics. "And now, if Eric catches on, she's in deep. Turns out, finding your girlfriend's hickey is not actually a 'snag from my purse' tends to raise questions, then we get Tegan flipping a table at Desert Bloom."

Claire gasped. "No!"

"It's all making sense now," I chirped in, swallowing my fifth breadstick and Lexi arched a brow, judging Tegan for her poor choices. "No wonder she went full Hulk last weekend," I said, recalling Tegan's table-flipping rage. "She's sweating it that Eric'll find out she's out here auditioning for *Fifty Shades of Senior Citizen*. The girl's got more secrets than

Armie Hammer's WhatsApp history."

Claire's eyes widened, darting between Lexi and me like we'd just suggested a karaoke night. "Wait—so Tegan's… *suicidal?*"

"No!" Lexi groaned, massaging her temples like Claire had just quoted TMZ as gospel. "She's either desperate for a Gucci handbag and willing to bang a grandad to get it, or she's got a kink for hearing aids. My money's on the first. Girl's hustling."

"Honestly?" I shuddered, picturing Eric's UFC-honed hands around Tegan's throat. "Maybe her Tesla payments piled up. VIP gigs don't pay like they used to—too many Insta wannabes undercutting the market."

Lexi nodded, sipping her strawberry lemonade like a CEO at a board meeting. "Spot on. She's figured that silver foxes are easier than hustling at the VIP section. Flash a bit of leg, laugh at their 'back in my day' stories, and bam— you're shopping the Plaza on his Amex. Risky? Sure. But Tegan's got the survival instincts of a wolf, that one."

I snorted. Lexi knew her stuff. If anyone could spot a sugar daddy a mile away, it was her.

"Felicia's gonna lose it when I tell her," I said, already mentally drafting the Messages novel.

Claire, now paler than an Alfredo refill, whispered, "This feels… dark."

"Nah," Lexi said, waving a manicured hand. "It's just Tuesday."

CHAPTER

THIRTEEN

"WHERE'S THE VIP AREA?" Lexi hissed, teetering on stilettos that sparkled like disco balls under the bar's rustic Edison bulbs. I yanked her arm before she could flag down a baffled bartender holding a tray of nachos.

"There is no VIP here," I muttered, steering her toward a sticky wooden table Felicia had claimed with the ferocity of a Black Friday shopper. "No velvet ropes, no bottle service, just… people. Enjoy it!"

Lexi blinked at the small room. "But where do we sit? Is there a list? A doorman? A tiny clipboard?!"

"Babe, this isn't the Wynn," Felicia said, rolling her eyes. "It's a downtown bar. You sit where there's space—or you stand and pray your heels survive the beer puddles." Then, she whispered, "You of all people should know a downtown bar when you see it."

Praying Lexi didn't hear the last bit, I pushed her in. Didn't want to start a fight mid-drink next to the pole place Lexi's mom was still known for her 'twirl and twerk' move.

The Griffin was my sanctuary—a cozy, unpretentious hole-in-the-wall where the only exclusive thing was the bartender's secret recipe for spicy margaritas. No influencers, no $1,000 champagne towers, just mismatched furniture and a jukebox playing *Arctic Monkeys* on loop.

Lexi, however, looked about as comfortable as a peacock in a pigeon coop.

"This table's got splinters," she whispered, recoiling from the wood like it might give her a fatal paper cut.

"It's called ambience," I said, shoving a cocktail into her hands. "Now drink your overpriced mojito and pretend you're slumming it for a charity dare."

Lexi sipped her drink, side-eyeing a group of young meat nearby—twenty-somethings in 501 jeans and artful stubble, laughing over pints of cheap beer. "Babies," she sniffed. "Do they even know what a mortgage is?"

Felicia snorted. "Doubt it. But that one's got abs like a bodybuilder. Go on, Lex—live a little. Trade diamonds for *denim*."

"Psh, I'd rather French-kiss a cactus," Lexi said,

smoothing her sequined mini-dress. "Youth is wasted on the young. They think 'generational wealth' is a TikTok trend."

I hid a grin. Lexi's obsession with silver foxes wasn't just about the money (though, let's be real—it mostly was). It was the power. The way those men hung on her every word, bought her Tiffany trinkets just because, and introduced her as their "younger, more vibrant model" at charity galas. To Lexi, dating a 65-year-old CEO wasn't gold-digging—it was curating a lifestyle.

"Admit it," I teased, nodding at the guys. "You're tempted."

"By *that*?" She gestured at a guy attempting a TikTok dance in loafers. "Please. I'd rather date an heir—a young one."

Felicia elbowed me, her whisper sharp as a tack. "Knew she wasn't just into antiques," she giggled, nodding at Lexi eyeing the snack table like it was a Nordstrom sale.

I snorted into my Aperol spritz—until Felicia gasped, her grip on my arm tighter than a denim jumpsuit. "Oh. My. God."

"What?" I hissed, craning my neck like a meerkat.

"It's him!"

My drink sloshed perilously close to my blouse. "Who?"

"Eric!"

I choked. There, across the room, was *the* Eric Mann—Tegan's UFC Dick Print, looking like he'd stepped out of a *GQ* spread titled "Casually Ripped."

Lexi glanced up from her drink, eyebrow arched like a TV judge. "*That's* Eric? The UFC wannabe you're meant to be stealing?"

"How do you even know him?" I whispered, panic rising.

Lexi smoothed her already perfect dress. "Eva, honestly. He's famous. Fights on stream. He's got a protein powder line startup. How've you missed telling me this?"

I gaped. Famous? Protein powder? I'd been flirting with a Z-list celeb and didn't even know? No wonder Tegan treated him like a Trophy Husband™. "I didn't know."

Lexi straightened, her posture shifting from hungover Sunday to *Love Island* bombshell. I'd seen this transformation before—Lexi, the huntress, ready to pounce.

"He's legit UFC, not a wannabe," she said, like I'd asked what a toaster was.

I stared at Eric, then at Lexi, then at my spritz. Right. So not only was he Tegan's boyfriend—he was Vegas' answer to *Rocky*. Great.

"You're telling me," I muttered, "I've been plotting to

swipe a man who's practically on billboards?"

Felicia smirked. "Girl, you've been living under a rock."

I glared. It wasn't like she knew, either.

"UFC or not, if Tegan's lurking here, I'm out," I hissed, clutching my Aperol like a stress ball. "I didn't stage a *Mission: Impossible* extraction to rescue Felicia from her shift just to bump into that lunatic in my happy place."

Lexi sipped her martini with the elegance of a Bond villain. "Honestly, cheating on Eric with Scott? That's like trading a vintage Bentley for a mobility scooter."

"A mobility scooter with a trust fund," Felicia added, grinning. "And a knack for unsolicited CPR, apparently."

I snorted, nearly mainlining my Aperol. "Imagine choosing Scott's erotic asphyxiation over Eric's… everything. It's like opting for a lukewarm Subway sandwich when there's a full Thanksgiving spread."

"Babe," Lexi purred, examining Eric's hands like they were auction lots, "those knuckles have seen things, I'm sure. I'd let him rearrange my internal organs if he asked—"

"Hi," said a voice behind us.

"—nicely." Lexi's head whipped around, her smile shifting from murderess to manic pixie dream girl in 0.2 seconds. "Hi! I'm Lexi. This—" she gestured grandly at me,

"—is Eva, and that's Felicia, our resident cinnamon roll. Loved your last UFC fight."

Felicia mouthed "cinnamon roll?!" as I froze, my brain blue-screening like a DMV computer. Eric stood there, all six-foot-something of him, looking like he'd just stepped out of a *Men's Health* cover shoot and into a rom-com directed by the universe to spite me.

Eric laughed at cinnamon roll. Or maybe at Lexi's organ rearranging comment, unsure. "I've had the pleasure of meeting Eva and Felicia."

"What a surprise," I said, a goofy smile plastered on my face.

"Didn't peg you for UFC fans," he said, his grin effortless and sweet.

"We're not! Just Lexi," I blurted. "We're just… avoiding our exes. And discussing niche hobbies. Yoga. Knitting. Tax evasion—"

Felicia kicked me under the table.

Eric raised an eyebrow. "Tax evasion's a hobby?"

"For some," Lexi said, shooting me a *shut up now* glare. "But we prefer contact sports. Jiu jitsu. Capybara (*did she mean Capoeira?*). Erotic asphyx—"

"Wine?" I barked, slamming my empty glass down.

"Anyone want wine? I'll get wine."

As I fled to the bar, I heard Lexi sigh, "Bless her heart, she's like a meerkat on espresso."

Eric's laugh followed me—warm, rumbly, and infuriatingly attractive. By the time I returned with a bottle of Pinot Gris (and an emergency shot of tequila for myself), Lexi had somehow roped him into debating the merits of "tactical choking" versus "recreational choking."

"—but if you're not using a safe word," she was saying, "you're basically playing Russian roulette with your trachea."

Eric, to his credit, looked equal parts amused and terrified. "Noted. I'll stick to sparring partners who *don't* want to murder me."

I slid into my seat, avoiding eye contact like he was a spoiler for *Love Is Blind*. But then he turned that smile on me, and my resolve crumbled faster than a gluten-free brownie.

Where's Tegan? I thought, half-dreading, half-hoping she'd burst in wielding a fire extinguisher and a subpoena. At least then I'd have an excuse to scream.

But for now, there was just Eric. And his stupid fighter's hands. And the sinking realization that my "revenge" plan now involved wanting to impress him with my knowledge of tax evasion.

As if summoned by Lexi's huntress-worthy pheromones, Eric's friends swaggered over—all cheesy grins and gym-toned bravado. Lexi, ever the flirt pro, pivoted seamlessly into their orbit, tossing out phrases like "VIP lounges are so 2022" and "nothing beats a downtown hole-in-the-wall bar." The guys—dressed like they'd raided a Ross sale—nodded along, lapping up her "I'm too high-class for this" charm.

Lexi said pro athletes had two fatal flaws: too much cash and too little life experience. (Translation: they were loaded man-children who couldn't spell "monogamy" if you spotted them the *M-O-N*.) And sure enough, these ones oozed UFC young-and-excited money—all Rolex wrists and locker-room banter. They probably thought Lexi was just another Botoxed gold-digger. Joke's on them—she was playing 4D chess while they were stuck on Snapchat.

But Eric? Eric was different. Not just because he wasn't eyeing Lexi like a $5 steak and lobster deal at a Station casino. Or because he laughed without constraints at Felicia's silly segues. No—it was the way he lingered in my peripheral vision, like an eye booger I couldn't ignore. Stupid, really. This was *meant* to be revenge, not a rom-com montage.

Then Felicia—bless her soul—leaned in. "Where's Tegan?"

Eric's brow twitched, a micro-flinch I'd noticed before. The man had a tell sharper than a Chili's steak knife.

"No clue," Eric said, shrugging with casual grace. "Why does she always ask me about Tegan?" He leaned in, his voice dipping to a conspiratorial whisper that smelled faintly of tequila and trouble.

I opened my mouth to say, *"Because boyfriends typically know where their girlfriends are?"* but Lexi materialized out of the ether, yanking me aside.

"I'm out," she announced, air-kissing my cheek so forcefully I felt a static shock. "See that man—" she nodded toward a guy across the bar who looked like he'd stepped out of a Hugo Boss ad crossed with a Golden Retriever, "—he has a Rolex *and* a six-pack. Duty calls."

"It's barely been an hour," I hissed. "What about Charles?"

Lexi waved a hand, her diamonds catching the light like a disco ball. "Charles thinks I'm at a yoga retreat. Namaste, darling."

And thinking I didn't care what geriatric Charles had to say, I threw, "Just don't let him do erotic asphyxiation on you," I muttered, referencing Scott-gate.

She gasped. "Eva!" Then, "It's free game if he's not a

target." With a wink, she vanished, leaving a trail of vanilla scent and poor life choices.

I turned back to the table, where a fresh Aperol spritz sat like a taunt from the universe. *Oh, this'll end well.*

Eric's friends had scattered—likely missing Lexi's energy—leaving him alone, thumbing his phone. Felicia, ever the traitor, mumbled something about "bathroom emergencies" and fled.

"So," Eric said, sliding into Lexi's vacated seat. "That dress."

"What about it?" I said, suddenly hyper-aware of his relative closeness.

"It's distracting." His grin was a lethal cocktail of charm and cheek. "And I don't think it's the dress making me feel this way."

I choked on my drink. *Was he…? No. Was I…?*

Flirting, in my world, was a carefully orchestrated ballet of hair flips and accidental eye contact. Not direct and to the point. I'd planned a slow-build, a few witty zingers over the net, a caress here and there, not have him spike the ball into my face.

"Thanks?" I squeaked, channeling the confidence of a damp lettuce leaf.

His smirk widened. "Relax. I don't bite. Unless you're into that."

Oh god. Was that a *Fifty Shades* reference? A UFC joke? A Taylor Swift lyric? My brain short-circuited, defaulting to panic-laughter.

Silence.

Let's be clear: Eric was *hot*. Like, Henry Cavill in his *Superman* era hot. And sure, I'd maybe—hypothetically—pictured him shirtless, wrestling sheets in my IKEA bed. But actually acting on it? With Tegan lurking like a TV judge with a grudge? Not. Likely.

First off, Tegan's rage made Amy Dunne (*Gone Girl* psychopath fit her, didn't it) look like an amateur. If she caught me sniffing around her man, I'd be found buried under a Target parking lot come Tuesday. Second, the man was sloppy seconds—and not just any old leftovers. We're talking "Tegan's into breath play" sloppy seconds. I'd sooner date a *Love Is Blind* unmarried than touch a man who'd survived her *Fifty Shades* auditions. *Shudder.*

And yeah, Eric was charming. Obnoxiously so. All smoldery gazes and biceps that could've been carved by a cake sculptor. But this wasn't about him. This was about winning. Or it had been, until he hit me with that floppy-haired rom-com line:

"Not to be too forward," he murmured, suddenly shy as a CVS cashier during a condom purchase, "but Saturdays at the café? It's not the coffee I go for. It's you."

Yikes. If he'd been some Tinder swipe after two shots, I'd have melted faster than a Magnum in July. I was meant to steal him anyway, make Tegan pay for all the hurt she'd caused. But it was too easy. Like stealing Haribo from a toddler. Where was the fun? The chase? The drama?

I froze, my face doing that deer in headlights thing. Eric noticed it instantly.

"Shit—that was too much, wasn't it?" He rubbed his neck, all bashful. "Blame the tequila."

"Eva!" Felicia bellowed, saving me from my existential spiral. "The guys are heading to Gold Spike! Wanna?"

"Pass," I said, still reeling. "You go. Tell them I've got… a thing."

Eric burned coals into my eyes. "Not coming, then?"

"Raincheck," I said, pulling away from him, suddenly all *Pride and Prejudice* indignant.

Flirting for revenge was one thing. But realizing Eric was about as challenging as a Connect 4 match? *Ugh.* Tegan could keep him.

CHAPTER

FOURTEEN

IT WAS A BEAUTIFUL morning, the sun was practically singing "Here Comes the Sun" in a passive-aggressive falsetto, as if Valentine's Day hadn't already commandeered every shop window with heart-shaped monstrosities and $15 "I wuff you" teddy bears. I inhaled the crisp air, determined to ignore the fact that my love life resembled a 3-for-1 deal—convenient, underwhelming, and best consumed alone.

"At least the weather's on my side," I muttered, squinting at a cloud shaped suspiciously like a Cupid's arrow. Thanks, universe. Subtle.

Pilates had left me sore and with the existential dread of someone who'd just paid $50 to "find her core." Normally, I'd soothe my bruised ego (and glutes) with a cortado at Desert Bloom Café. But today, the café felt like navigating a *Housewives* reunion—terrifying, humiliating, and likely to end with someone crying into a panini.

All because of Eric.

Eric, who'd confessed over tequila last night that he "couldn't stop thinking about me." Eric, who'd looked at me like I was the only person on Earth. Eric, who'd apparently mistaken our flirty banter for a *Married at First Sight* audition.

I'd envisioned my revenge as a sleek, cinematic masterpiece—me swooping in, stealing Tegan's man with a smoldering glance, and sauntering off as she wept into her Tesla's leather seats. Instead, it played out like a Sundance drama project: awkward pauses, misplaced laughter, and a climactic scene where I tripped over a barstool yelling, "It's fine, I'm fine!" And Tegan's missed 90% of it.

Worst of all? Eric hadn't even hesitated. Turns out, my grand scheme to weaponize him had backfired spectacularly. Instead of "making Tegan pay," I'd accidentally signed up for a masterclass in How to Be the Side Chick.

"Rude," I huffed. All week, I'd deluded myself into thinking Eric was different—a gentle giant with the soul of a Mr. Rogers narrator. But no. He was just another guy with nice arms and the moral compass of a pirate.

Even Pilates couldn't stretch the ick away.

"You alright?" Felicia said behind the counter. "You've

been glaring at the door for five minutes."

I groaned, leaning on the counter. "Eric's an idiot."

"Obviously," she said, cleaning the space. "But he's an idiot with a six-pack and Tegan for girlfriend. Priorities, babe. Take your revenge, but don't get too involved."

"He looked at me like I was a Costco sample on a Sunday. Temporary. Disposable. Reduced to clearance."

Felicia snorted. "So? Use him back. Crash his car. Steal his gym socks. Key 'Eva wuz here' into his car."

"That's your solution? Vandalism?"

"It's Valentine's Week! Channel your inner *Bridget Jones*. Burn his pants. Sing "Obsessed" naked. Live!"

I laughed, despite myself. "You're a menace."

"And you're overcomplicating this," she said. "Eric's not a pawn. He's a blip in the radar. Tegan's the endgame."

"The endgame?" Had I been overthinking this? Or maybe, I'd become emotionally involved.

"Yup. It's not Eric, is it. It never was. Tegan's the endgame."

"Screw this," I muttered. "Not letting some guy with the moral depth of a puddle ruin my Saturday routine."

I flopped into my window seat—the one where the sun

hit like a spotlight—and tried to read. But my brain was too busy replaying last night's horror show. Eric's puppy-dog eyes. Me, stuck in a telenovela with a wonky plot twist.

Let's be clear: I hadn't signed up to be Eric's sneaky link. This was supposed to be a tactical flirtation—a swift, surgical strike on Tegan's ego, not a *Cheaters* audition. But no. Eric had swooped into my trap like a Labrador into a paddling pool, blissfully unaware he was meant to be a prop, not a participant. Honestly, men should come with subtitles.

"He should've known," I'd ranted to Felicia at 2 a.m., slurping emergency Ben & Jerry's straight from the tub. "This wasn't a rom-com meet-cute! It was espionage! James Bond doesn't accidentally fall for the villain's girlfriend while defusing a bomb!"

Felicia, bless her, had nodded along, sleep-tired eyes and all. "He's a dick, Eva, not just the print. His brain's just a screensaver of bicep curls and protein shakes. Cut him some slack."

But still. Tegan had swiped my ex like a hacked Netflix account, and now her upgrade was sliding into my DMs with the subtlety of a failed reality star. Where was my righteous triumph? My "How do you like them apples, Tegan?!" moment? Instead, I felt like I'd licked a used tube of lip gloss —sticky, regretful, and vaguely ashamed.

Felicia, of course, had leaned into the chaos. After abandoning Eric's "boys' night" at Gold Spike, she'd dissected his every move like Sherlock in a sequin skirt.

"He called you 'low-key gorgeous,'" she'd said, snorting. "*Low-key?* Babe, if a man ever describes you as 'low-key' anything, throw his phone into the Bellagio."

Now, nursing a cortado at the café, I grimaced. "Low-key my ass. Look at the text he sent me at 3 a.m."

Felicia read. "Oh, fuck." And then she smirked. "And yet," Felicia said, nodding at Eric's latest DM—a winky-face emoji beside a "U up?"—"here we are."

"This isn't what I was hoping for."

"Well, it's what you got, so what are you gonna do about it?"

She flitted off to handle the mid-morning rush, leaving me to glare at my phone. Eric's profile photo—a gym selfie with a sweaty top—smiled back, oblivious.

Fine. So Plan A (Destroy Tegan) had morphed into Plan B (Avoid Becoming a Sneaky Link Subplot). But as I deleted his message, a thought struck me: maybe the sweetest revenge wasn't stealing Tegan's man. Maybe it was letting her keep him.

Tegan could have her six-pack trophy. I'd take a cortado

and a clean conscience, thank you.

The door chimed, and I glanced up reflexively. *Please don't let it be him.* But there he was—Eric, composed and unfazed, as if last night's awkwardness had never happened. Our eyes met briefly, and I looked away, a flicker of regret surfacing. Felicia's advice to "have fun" suddenly felt reckless. Maybe I'd pushed things further than I'd meant to.

"Eva," he said warmly, his smile effortless.

"Hi, Eric," I replied, my tone polite but distant. Whatever game I'd been playing, the thrill had faded. What started as harmless banter now felt tangled, and I wanted out.

He paused, sensing my hesitation. "About last night… I crossed a line. I'm sorry if I made you uncomfortable. I just want us to be friendly, that's all."

I straightened, folding my hands neatly. "Apology accepted. But let's keep things simple, okay? No need for anything more."

He blinked, caught off guard. "Right. I didn't realize it came off that way, but sure. Got it."

I nodded and turned back to my book, though my focus wavered. Annoyance prickled—not at him, but at myself. Using him to rattle Tegan had felt clever at first, but now it just left me feeling uneasy in the worst way.

He lingered for a moment, then left without ordering. I watched him go, his absence leaving a quiet hollowness. For a second, I wondered if I'd been too harsh—but the sight of Tegan's Tesla in the parking lot steadied me. Today, at least, I'd dodged a mess of my own making.

"Holy crap!" Lexi's fork clattered onto her plate during lunch, her eyes wide as a *Game of Thrones* cliffhanger. "Eric Mann? *The* Eric Mann? Six-foot-something of 'I-do-crossfit-on-my-days-off' Eric Mann wants you?" She leaned in, her lashes fluttering. "I mean, obviously he does, darling! But *wow*. The man's got taste. Shame it's morally bankrupt taste."

I stabbed a cherry tomato. "It wasn't supposed to be real, Lex. It was a performance, a dance, a heist. Like one of those thirst traps where everyone's fully clothed and emotionally stunted."

Claire, ever the human equivalent of a weighted blanket, patted my hand. "They're both trash, Eva. Tegan's a landfill fire, and Eric's the seagull circling it. Let them have each other."

Lexi laughed. "But where's the fun in that? And what does it make you, wanting to steal him in the first place? Just because you changed your mind after rattling him, it doesn't make you Miss Innocent." She waved her strawberry lemonade, sloshing some onto the tablecloth. "Or are you exempt because of karma?"

"It was just a plan, not a life mantra." Stealing was Tegan's thing. "And it's not karma," I muttered, "it's payback. And I'm done."

"Oh, come on," Lexi pressed. "You literally started this! You batted those Bambi eyes, you laugh-giggled at his deadlift stories—don't think I didn't notice!"

"Did not," I grumbled. But she was right. I'd started it all.

"Look on the bright side," Lexi said. "Maybe they have an open relationship and no one's doing a naughty."

Claire snorted. "No one does open relationships. Eva's right. This whole thing is wrong."

"Thank you," I said, pointing my fork at her. "And newsflash—if Tegan and Eric had some cozy open relationship, she wouldn't have gone full *Exorcist* when she saw us chatting. That wasn't jealousy, that was possession. The woman's got a hoarding problem—men, secrets, cringy sex acts."

Claire nodded sagely. "Exactly. She stole your boyfriend like he was a TJ Maxx handbag. You think she wants you swimming around Dick Print?"

"Bringing back the Dick Print, I like it."

Lexi fake-swooned. "It's poetic, really. You could be her reckoning, Eva! Her comeuppance!"

"Or," Claire interjected, "you could be smart and let them marinate in their own toxic soup. Pass the bread?"

Claire's words landed like a sucker punch to the gut.

"Shit," I muttered, the truth of it slicing through me. "You're right. Tegan's been coiled tighter than a viper around me. Like she's just waiting for the universe to drop an anvil on her head for all the crap she's pulled. Maybe guilt's finally rotting her from the inside out."

Lexi barked a laugh, sharp and unhinged. "Oh, please steal Eric. God, I'd pay to watch her implode. UFC fighter? Vegas's golden boy? She's probably already planning their 'power couple' hashtag. Imagine her face when he dumps her basic ass for *you*." She leaned in, eyes glittering like broken glass. "What'd that twat she stole from you even do? Sell used cars? Exactly. This isn't revenge, Eva—it's art."

Claire snorted, her usual sweetness tinged with something darker. "I mean... she's not wrong. Tegan's karma's overdue."

"I'm not stealing him!" I snapped, though the lie burned my tongue. The idea clawed at me—fantasies of Tegan's perfect life splintering, Eric's hands on my hips instead of hers. But I shoved it down. "It's gross. He's tainted. You think I want her sloppy seconds? Her erotic asphyxiation leftovers?"

Lexi rolled her eyes, slamming her glass down. "Stop pretending you're above this. You crave that payback. And Eric? He's not some charity case—he's a trophy. You could ruin her with a flirty text. So do it."

Claire's smile turned sly. "Or… don't. But let's not pretend it wouldn't be a little fun."

I gripped the edge of the table, my nails biting into the wood. "It's not about fun. It's about not becoming her."

"Boring," Lexi drawled, flicking her hair. "You're sitting on a grenade and refusing to pull the pin. But fine. Be a martyr. Just know—" She leaned closer, her voice a serpent's hiss. "—you could break her. One smile, and Eric's yours. And that's a win, whether you admit it or not."

The room buzzed with tension, thick and sweet as poison. Claire's quiet chuckle. Lexi's manic grin. My pulse roaring in my ears.

Then, like a snapped rubber band, we burst into laughter —wild, jagged, cathartic. Jokes about Tegan's overfilled lips, Eric's gym selfies, the way she'd literally trademarked her own initials. For once, the power was ours.

But under the laughter, the truth hummed: I wanted to. Not for Eric. For the chaos. For the look on her face.

And that scared me more than anything.

CHAPTER
FIFTEEN

"I HAVE NEWS," LEXI announced, slamming the clinic door open like she was storming the stage at a Beyoncé freebie. Her normally sleek dark hair resembled a bird's nest, and her eyeliner had migrated south to her cheekbones. It was all very off-brand.

I gaped. "Did you sleep in a bush?"

"Priorities, Eva!" She flopped into a patient chair, her designer handbag emitting a suspicious clink of empty mini-wine bottles. "Tegan's gone full sugar baby. Scott's paying her a mortgage-sized allowance to be his 24/7 'companion.'" She air-quoted companion like it meant "human Tamagotchi."

I choked. "But she's with Eric! Unless—"

"Unless they're polyamorous?" Lexi snorted.

"Tegan's about as polyamorous as Jane Bennet. She's

just greedy."

"Well, she's something because she's definitely Scott's sugar baby."

My brain short-circuited. "So she's dating Eric *and* monetizing Scott's midlife crisis? How's she juggling that? Time travel? Clones?"

"Men are easy to juggle when they're all narcissists with gold cards," Lexi said, inspecting her chipped manicure. "Old ones especially. They're too busy Googling 'how to screenshot' to notice you're double-dipping."

I frowned. "But you've got Charles. How's that going?"

Lexi's smile froze, her Botox fighting for its life. "Charles is fine. A bit clingy since he discovered emojis. Keeps sending me eggplants and water droplets. Anyway—" She bulldozed on, "—Tegan's raking in six figures to watch Scott nap in his yacht. Six. Figures. For *nap supervision*."

"Is the nap before or after the erotic asphyxiation?" I said, laughing and imagining Tegan charging hourly rates to nod at Scott's stories about his golf handicap, finger marks on her throat.

"After, I'm sure," Lexi said, her face all runny mascara and sourpuss cringes.

"But what about Eric? I wonder if he knows."

Lexi waved a hand. "Eric's probably too busy bench-pressing his insecurities to notice. Or maybe he's got a sugar granny on the side. Who cares? Point is, Tegan's winning at capitalism, and we're here labeling syringes like peasants. Do you even know how long it took me to sign Charles?"

"I'm guessing not a few weeks?"

"Almost a year!"

"Shit," I said, mad I was impressed by Tegan's luck. "All those rules for nothing."

She huffed and flounced out, leaving a cloud of vanilla perfume and existential dread.

I stared at the wall, where a motivational poster of a kitten dangling from a clipboard read "Hang in there!"

"Hang in there," I muttered. "Or just marry the Crypt Keeper. Whatever."

As I sanitized a tray of instruments, I couldn't decide what horrified me more: Tegan's transactional love life, or the fact that Lexi now considered her a career icon.

Some days, adulthood felt less like *Bridget Jones* and more like *Black Mirror*—if *Black Mirror* were sponsored by Tinder and featured a soundtrack of men explaining Bitcoin.

The drive to the café was autopilot—until Tegan's Tesla lunged at me like a shark spotting blood. Her car screeched out of the lot, swerving so violently I yanked the wheel hard, my gaudy green car fishtailing.

"Fucking psycho!" I screamed, slamming the horn. She tore off down the road, tires smoking, weaving through traffic like *Grand Theft Auto* on crack.

Nice, Tegan. Real subtle.

Felicia's text buzzed: "Get in here. Shane's late. I've got TEA."

I stormed inside, still shaking, only to find Felicia practically vibrating behind the counter. Her eyes locked on me, wild.

"Eva! You just missed everything," she hissed, dragging me to my table like a kidnapper with a gossip addiction.

"Let me guess—Tegan's auditioning for *Fast & Furious 22*?" I snapped, still tasting adrenaline.

"Both of them! Eric and Tegan, here together."

"Both?"

She leaned in, voice dropping to a whisper-shout. "Eric

walks in, cool as a mannequin, orders his usual. I'm steaming milk, playing it chill, right? Then—*bam!*—Tegan slams through the door like the Kool-Aid Man on steroids. Glaring at him like he'd just keyed her Tesla."

I nearly choked. "And?"

Felicia mimed an explosion. "Eric turns around—*boom*—'It's over.' Just like that. No warning. Tegan goes nuclear—screaming about loyalty, throwing his cappuccino at the wall. He didn't even flinch, he's so used to her outbursts, probably. Says she's 'distracting the new guys.' She goes on another rant, begging, poor thing. Then he says 'Tegan, please. You're embarrassing yourself,' and walked out. Left her there practically sobbing in latte foam."

My jaw hit the floor. "He dumped her?"

"Dumped? Babe, he nuked her. Right in front of the whole café." Felicia's grin was feral. "Best part? He glanced at your empty table on his way out. Twice."

The world tilted. *He knew.* Knew about Scott. Knew about everything. And he'd chosen today—the day Tegan nearly pancaked me—to detonate her life.

Felicia slid my cortado across the table, her smirk dripping with mischief. "Karma's a bitch, huh?"

I sipped my coffee, bitterness mingling with sweet, sweet

vindication. Outside, the sun blazed like the universe itself was cackling.

Felicia's eyes went wider than a whoopsie cushion. "I think I know karma, and her name is Eva."

"I had nothing to do with that," I said, half hoping, half wishing.

"Didn't you?"

"Lexi told me Tegan's on Scott's payroll now. Sugar baby status. Six figures to watch him nap in cashmere socks after a choking session."

Felicia gasped, clutching her chest. "*No*. So that's why Eric's gone full Hulk? Because Tegan's monetizing her TFMAM (Trust Fund Middle-Aged Man™) while he's stuck bench-pressing his feelings?!"

"Lexi thinks they're open."

"Open, my ass. Have you seen how jealous Tegan is?"

"Exactly!" I said, feeling like Sherlock in hospital scrubs. "But here's the kicker—if their relationship *is* open, why's Tegan throwing a tantrum over Eric flirting with *me*? And why's Eric mad about Scott? It's like they're playing Mario Kart but only Tegan gets the banana peels."

Felicia snorted, nearly inhaling flour from her apron. "Because, duh—*if* they're open, Tegan's fine with Eric necking randos, just not *you*. You're her kryptonite. Her expired coupon. Her Uber Eats order that never arrives."

I nodded, trying to untangle the mess like sheets after a spin cycle. "So Eric's mad because... Tegan's getting paid? Or because she's doing weird sex acts? Or—"

"Or because he's realized he's dating a human vending machine?" Felicia interjected, shrugging. "Who knows? Maybe they were never open—just sneaking around like teenagers with a fake ID. Either way, it's a dumpster fire, and I'm here for the popcorn."

"Honestly, I don't care," I said, shaking my head. "As long as I'm not the one holding the fire extinguisher, they can burn it all down for all I care. This is way too much drama for a Tuesday."

"Amen to that," Felicia agreed, before leaning in with a mischievous grin. "But real talk—what does it take to become a sugar baby? Asking for a friend."

I raised an eyebrow. "You? A sugar baby? I mean, Lexi's got a list of eligible Crypt Keepers. I hear Ty's still single— and he has a yacht."

Felicia shoved me playfully. "Hard pass. I'd rather date Nosferatu."

As she sauntered off to grab my tart, my brain kept

circling back to the same question: Why would Tegan sign up to be Scott's sugar baby when she had Eric?

I mean, sure, money's money—but Tegan's not exactly scraping pennies together. She's got the Tesla, the designer handbags, the VIP bottle service gig. So what's the angle?

Unless…

Unless it's not about the money.

I sipped my coffee, the pieces clicking into place. Tegan's not just after cash—she's after security. She's pushing thirty (like me, *cough, cough*), and maybe she's realized that serving champagne to men with neck wattles isn't a long-term career plan. Scott's her exit strategy—a cushy retirement fund wrapped in a Burberry trench coat.

But then there's Eric.

Eric, who's basically a rom-com hero with a six-pack and a dental plan. Eric, who should be enough for anyone. But if he's sliding into my DMs while Tegan's out here auctioning off her weekends to Scott, maybe he's not as perfect as I thought.

"Here's your tart," Felicia said, sliding a raspberry pastry across the table. "And your existential crisis, served with a side of whipped cream."

I groaned. "Why is dating so hard? Why can't it just be

easy? Like, meet a nice guy, fall in love, argue over whose turn it is to unload the dishwasher—"

"—and not have to worry about his sugar baby ex showing up at your Pilates class?" Felicia finished, grinning. "Dream big, babe."

As I bit into the tart, a nagging thought crossed my mind. Maybe Eric's not the hero of this story. Maybe he's just another guy with nice arms and questionable morals.

Maybe he was just perfect in my mind and nowhere else.

Because if there's one thing I've learned, it's this: life's too short to waste on men who can't decide if they're in an open relationship or a Target parking lot.

CHAPTER

SIXTEEN

———

"LEXI," I SAID, STABBING a forkful of pasta with more force than intended. "What's going on? You've been glued to your phone, and you haven't mentioned Charles in days. Spill."

Lexi froze mid-bite, her fork hovering like a helicopter over a crime scene. "Nothing's going on," she said, shoveling pasta into her mouth like it was a hostage situation.

Claire leaned in, her eyes narrowing like a detective in a *Law&Order: SVU* episode. "Don't lie. You're blushing. You're distracted. And you haven't once mentioned your 'long-term financial strategy'—which, FYI, is code for 'marry a Crypt Keeper.' So, what gives?"

"Oh, come on," Lexi groaned, rolling her eyes. "You're being dramatic."

"Dramatic?" I said, feigning offense. "You roped me into

flirting with a *septuagenarian* to keep Charles happy, and now you're ghosting us? Not cool, Lex. Not cool."

Lexi sighed, pushing her plate away. "Fine. I broke up with Charles."

The table fell silent. Even the background chatter of the restaurant seemed to pause, as if the universe itself was gasping.

"What?" Claire and I said in unison.

Lexi shrugged, her usual sparkle dimmed. "He proposed. With a prenup. An ironclad prenup." She spat the word like it was a rogue olive pit. "After a year of my life, he thinks I'm going to sign away my future for a man who still uses Yahoo Mail? Please."

I blinked, stunned. "He proposed? And you said *no*?"

"I said *hell no*," Lexi corrected, her voice sharp. "I'm not spending the best years of my life arguing over which one of his spoiled kids gets the Hamptons house while he Googles 'best adult diapers.'"

Claire reached across the table, squeezing Lexi's hand. "I'm sorry, Lex. That's… rough."

"It's fine," Lexi said, though her smile didn't reach her eyes. "I mean, he was never going to marry me without strings. I just thought I was worth more than a legal document to him."

I felt a pang of guilt for pushing her. "Lex, I had no idea. I'm so sorry."

She waved a hand, her diamonds catching the light. "Don't be. I'm fine. Honestly, I'm better off. Who needs a man with a yacht when I've got *me*?"

Claire raised her glass. "To Lexi. May her next target have a heart—and an aversion to prenups."

We clinked glasses, but as Lexi forced a laugh, I couldn't shake the feeling that her sparkle was a little dimmer than usual.

Playing devil's advocate, I said, "What's the prenup say, anyway?"

"Ten *thousand* dollars," Lexi spat, stabbing her fork into her pasta. "That's what his prenup offered. Ten grand. For marriage. I swallowed three of those the night you ditched me at XS."

The Ono drinks she'd gulped. I laughed, remembering.

Claire and I exchanged a glance, the kind you reserve for watching a meltdown unfold in real time.

"He's paranoid," Lexi ranted, her voice sharp enough to cut glass. "Wants to 'protect his assets'—like I'm some gold-digging harlot. Meanwhile, he drops more than that on me monthly just to keep me around. But marriage? Oh no, that's where he draws the line. Idiot."

Claire shrugged, twirling her spaghetti. "I mean… why else would you be with him? It's not like he's winning personality awards."

Lexi shot her a glare that could've melted steel. "Exactly. The money's the point. But no, he's listening to his financial advisor and his lawyers like they're relationship gurus. Newsflash, Charles: your spreadsheets don't know me. And if he keeps this up, he'll be single faster than you can say 'alimony.'"

She shoved another forkful of pasta into her mouth, chewing like she was imagining it was Charles's ego. "And then there's Tegan," she added, her tone dripping with venom. "Waltzes in, bats her lashes at Scott, and suddenly they're talking marriage? No prenup? After a couple of months? Meanwhile, I've been with Charles for a year, and he's still clutching his wallet like it's Fort Knox."

"Fucking Tegan," I muttered, my own bitterness bubbling up. She had a knack for crashing into lives like a bowling ball.

Lexi's laugh was sharp, brittle. "I introduced them. *Me.* Like some kind of idiot matchmaker. And now she's living my dream while I'm stuck arguing with a man who thinks ten grand is a fair trade for my beauty and youth."

She slammed her fork down, her eyes blazing. "So I dumped him. Let him find some basic girl who'll settle for crumbs. I'm done." She pointed a finger at me, intense. "And don't be fooled. He'll find one. They're always out there."

The table fell silent, the weight of her words hanging in the air. Lexi, for all her bravado, looked… tired.

"Good for you," Claire said, her voice warm but firm. "Know your worth and don't settle. I did the same with my husband. When he said he wasn't sure about us, I packed my bags and left. Two days later, he was on my doorstep with an Albertsons bouquet and a speech about how he'd been a dimwit. Now look at us." She rubbed her baby bump, her smile soft. "When this little one arrives, our family will be complete. Don't settle for less than that, Lex."

Lexi sighed, stabbing a piece of pasta. "All I wanted was a guarantee of ten million if things went tits up. Is that so much to ask?"

"Ten million?!" I choked on my lemonade. I knew Charles was loaded, but that loaded?

"It's not even half his net worth," Lexi said, rolling her eyes. "It's pocket change to him. But no, he wants me to sign a prenup tighter than his Spanx. His lawyers are like *Shark Tank* meets *Suits*. It's exhausting. And now Scott's talking about marrying Tegan—no prenup, too."

Claire leaned back, her salad fork paused mid-air. "Well, I'm a fucking idiot, then. My husband proposed with a Ring Pop and a promise to split the laundry duties."

"Wait, *what*?" I said, my brain catching up. "Scott and Tegan are getting married? I thought she was just his sugar baby!"

Lexi shrugged, twirling her pasta. "Scott mentioned it to Charles. Apparently, Tegan's erotic asphyxiation on the first date strategy paid off. Who knew choking was the new meet-cute?"

I groaned. "No wonder Eric lost it at the café. He's probably realized he's dating a human coin flip."

"Maybe," Lexi said, her smirk returning. "But honestly, I'm done with Charles. He wouldn't even listen to me about the prenup. So, I met Brody—Eric's friend from the bar— and, well…" Her cheeks flushed. "He's not rich. He's not old. But he's nice. And he actually listens to me. We're seeing each other on Valentine's Day."

Claire gasped. "Lexi! That's huge! Brody's, like, normal. Are you happy?"

Lexi's smile widened as she pulled her pasta closer. "Yeah. I think I am. It's weird, but nice. Like, *really* nice. And I don't have to yell or say things twice, either."

As she dug into her meal, I couldn't help but smile. Lexi, the queen of gold-digging, had traded her Dubai Porta Potty dreams for a guy who probably owned one decent pair of boxers.

And honestly? It suited her.

"So you like Brody," I said, smirking. It wasn't a question—her face had lit up like a Black Friday sale at Macy's the second his name left her lips. "Maybe I'll see you at the café instead of Tegan soon."

Her smile faltered, and I instantly regretted the jab. "I don't know what I'm doing," she admitted, her voice softer now. "I just… I can't picture myself stuck in that café every day like you and Felicia."

Ouch. I swallowed the sting and forced a grin. "Well, Felicia's got a Valentine's date. So, guess who's the lone loser this year? Me." I pouted dramatically, though honestly, Valentine's Day was just Wednesday with extra chocolate.

Claire chimed in, her tone light. "I'll be home with a tub of Ben & Jerry's and my feet up. Solidarity, yeah?"

We laughed, and weirdly, it did make me feel better.

Later, I was neck-deep in bubbles and Pinot Grigio when Cali called. I grabbed my phone, balancing it precariously on the edge of the tub.

"Got some news for you," she said, her voice bubbling with excitement.

"Please tell me it's not a *Fifty Shades* update," I joked. "Won't be able to handle another vivid mental image."

"Sorry, I'm not Tegan," she shot back, and we both cackled. "But seriously… I'm pregnant!"

"Cali!" I squealed, nearly dropping my wine. "That's amazing! Rubi's going to be the best big sister."

We gushed for a while—Cali detailing Rubi's lack of reaction (babies, am I right?) and me pretending not to cry into my bubbles.

After we hung up, I sank back into the tub, swirling my wine. Life was weird. Felicia had a date. Lexi was swooning over Brody. Claire was glowing with impending motherhood. And Cali? Soon to be a mom of two.

My friends were thriving, and I was here. Soaking in a tub, wondering when my life would stop feeling like a Netflix series stuck on pause.

But for now, I raised my glass to the bubbles. "Cheers to something," I muttered. "Whenever it shows up."

CHAPTER

SEVENTEEN

"SHOULD I WEAR THE black or the blue?" Felicia demanded, thrusting two dresses under my nose. They were identical—same spaghetti straps, same *I'm definitely not from Shein* sheen—except one was the color of midnight, the other the exact shade of I-can-hide-a-stain-better.

"They're the same dress," I said, squinting.

"Eva," she groaned, flopping onto my bed like a disgraced Tinder swipe left alone for the night. "This is my first date since the Incident."

Ah, *the Incident*—a Tinder catastrophe involving a man who'd introduced his cat as "Calexit"—one of those California transplants that talked nothing but "California does this different" and "the food in California is better," and blah blah blah—and argued that *Love Actually* actually was "overrated." Felicia had had enough of him mid-pizza, but left home with him anyway, having one of "the worst" one-nighters she'd ever had. The next morning he'd texted her 17 voice notes about California weather and traffic and something or other. We didn't talk about the Incident.

"You'll look banging in either," I said, really meaning it —and not because the dresses were identical, either. "Unless you're planning on erotic asphyxiation. Then maybe the blue. Perfect shade of—"

Felicia hurled a cushion at me. "This is why you're single."

"Rude," I said, ducking. "But true."

She opted for the black ("Slimming!" she insisted, though she's built like an hourglass) and left in a haze of body spray, abandoning me on Valentine's.

Alone.

On. Valentine's.

Lexi was off rom-com-ing with Brody, Eric's UFC friend who apparently "loves rom-coms and doesn't own a single Rolex." Not hard to believe about some up-and-comer who was even less popular than Eric. Claire was home with a tub of Ben & Jerry's "Netflix & Chill'd" (which, let's be real, is just cookie dough with a side of existential dread, and maybe her husband on the side talking her ear off at the best parts of *Bridgerton*). And Cali? Flooding Instagram with #Blessed snaps of her toddler finger-painting rice onto their new rug.

So I did what any self-respecting, Richard Curtis-indoctrinated singleton would do: I slicked on brown lip liner, Googled "where to do single Valentine's" and marched downtown, to Fremont Street.

Now, Fremont on a Saturday night isn't for the faint-hearted. It's a kaleidoscope of neon, foot-tall drinks, and a guy dressed as a T-Rex murdering "Wonderwall" on a ukulele. The air reeked of regret, Heart Attack Grill oily fries, and the faint hope that a rogue double-decker might mow down the "Free Hugs!" guy and his suspect clipboard.

I wobbled past a bachelorette in "Bridezilla or Bust" sashes, a man offering Life Advice ($5 or a taco), and a pub called Liquor Up & Down where the floor's stickier than Duck Tape.

"Nice shoes!" slurred a guy in an I Heart Vegas jersey, swaying like a willow.

"Thanks!" I said, power-walking past.

"Wanna see my tramp stamp?"

"Pass!"

I slipped into the mermaid-themed bar—a glittering relic from the '90s, where the slot machines hummed like disgruntled bees and the air smelled vaguely of stale optimism. "One Valentine's Special, please," I announced to the bartender, who slid me a neon shot glass swimming with gummy bears and a fried Oreo dusted in heart-shaped sprinkles. Classy for $5. I claimed a sticky window seat, where I could people-watch and silently critique Fremont Street's finest: a man in head-to-toe sequins belting "Livin' on a Prayer," a woman in light-up heels attempting to line dance atop a table, and a group of guys dressed as Roman gladiators, all shirtless and sweat drips.

Outside, chaos reigned. But inside? For the first time all night, I felt content. Maybe it was the sugar rush. Maybe it was the cover band killing Justin Bieber. Or maybe it was the realization that being single on Valentine's Day meant no pressure to share my fried Oreo.

Single on Valentine's? I toasted my reflection in the grimy window. *Cheers to that.*

But Vegas peace is fleeting. Time to bolt before the crowd morphed into a sea of vodka-fueled Romeo wannabes. I clenched my keys between my knuckles—*thanks, Dad*—and wove through the throng, side-eyeing everyone like a pro.

"Need company, sweetheart?" slurred a man in a "Kiss Me, I'm Irish" shirt.

I whirled, Oreo crumbs clinging to my gloss. "Only if

you've got a platinum card and a therapist on speed dial."

His friends roared. He shuffled off.

I was halfway to my car when—

"Eva!"

I turned. There he stood, Eric. Eric, in a silly pajama suit-set and a heart-print bucket hat, clutching a fluorescent cocktail the size of a Labrador. Eric, jogging toward me like I was the last 7-Eleven sandwich at a gas station.

"Eva!" he repeated, slightly breathless (and possibly tipsy). "What a surprise seeing you!"

Behind him, his friends chanted "Shots! Shots!" while attempting to balance pint glasses on their heads. Brody, notably absent, was probably enjoying a normal Valentine's date with Lexi—candlelit, sans Roman gladiators.

"Eric," I said, casually shielding my leftover Oreo (it was huge) like it was state secrets. "What a nice surprise."

"This place is wild, isn't it?" He grinned, gesturing to a man dressed as Cupid riding a mechanical bull. "I like downtown. The Strip's too polished. This place has character."

I bit back a laugh. "Character, or a contact high from the slot machine fumes?"

He leaned in, eyes twinkling. "Both."

Before I could respond, Eric yanked me into a hug. Not one of those polite, "Oh-lovely-to-see-you-please-don't-stab-me" half-armed clutches. A full-on, chest-to-chest-pelvis-to-pelvis kind of hug—awkwardly intimate and weirdly committed.

For a solid three seconds, I froze. His cologne hit me like a rogue spray tan to the face. His stubble grazed my cheek, and I swear I felt his heartbeat thudding. The kind of hug that makes you forget you're clutching fried Oreo leftovers and a fluorescent slushy that's 90% Red 40.

Then, just as quickly, he pulled away, leaving me blinking like I'd just been flash-banged by a rom-com director.

"Sorry," he said, scratching his neck like he'd just remembered I'd told him to stay away. "I just… missed you."

Missed me?

I gaped at him. Was this flirting? Or had his UFC brain cells gotten scrambled during sparring? "Uh," I said, channeling my inner Shakespeare.

He grinned, eyes crinkling at the corners. "You look like you've seen a ghost."

"More like a heart-shaped hat," I shot back, gesturing to his accessory. "Did you raid a Claire's clearance aisle? Or is this part of your 'I'm a sensitive UFC sweetheart' rebrand?"

He laughed, undeterred. "You're one to talk. Is that glitter in your hair?"

"Defensive sparkles," I said, brushing my shoulder. "For repelling unsolicited hugs."

Around us, Fremont Street buzzed—but it all evaporated into nothing else but him and me.

Eric leaned in, his smirk curling the corner of his lips. "Admit it. You missed me too, Little Eva."

I stepped back, nearly tripping over a rogue beer can. "*Little Eva?* Are you giving me nicknames now? Or just trying to make me feel like an H&M mannequin next to your Savile Row cosplay?"

His grin widened. "How did you know? It's a pajama set, look." He pulled the pajama suit near me, begging me to touch.

"I can actually tell. It was a well panned out joke, only you've missed it."

"I haven't missed it, you see. I only wanted to get a little closer to you, is all."

He glanced down, and I seized the moment to retreat. His hug had left me dizzy, confused and bothered. But then it hit me—the memory of Tegan's screech at the café, her talon-like nails digging into his arm, begging him not to leave her.

Oh, fuck. Reality check.

I kept walking, Eric keeping up. "I'm leaving now," I said.

"I'm following. Just to make sure you get to you car safe," he said, raising his hands. In the elevator, our hands brushed, and I swear he sighed.

Sigh. In another life, maybe.

Once at the parking lot, Eric in tow, my car was not cooperating. I crouched beside the deflated tire, my phone clutched in my hand like a lifeline—except it was dead. Completely, utterly dead. You see, in the midst of my single-at-Valentine's-Day-anxiety, I'd forgotten to plug my phone in to at least 50%.

"Need a knight in slightly rumpled armor? Or perhaps pajama armor would be better said."

"Only if he's got a tire iron and a PhD in roadside rescues," I shot back, wiping fried Oreo grease from my face.

Eric laughed, the sound low and slightly slurred. "I've got a loyalty card for Tropical Smoothie and a receipt from 2017. Close enough?"

"Perfect," I said, thinking how was I going to call a tow.

Or an Uber.

Eric leaned against a lamppost, his pajama jacket slung over one shoulder and his combination tie and top loosened. His eyes glazed over, and that ridiculous drink in his hand suddenly became larger. "I'll take you home. Problem solved."

"You're hammered," I said flatly. "Go home before you trip into a drain."

"Hammered?" He scrunched his face. "I'm festively hydrated, if anything. These drinks have the alcohol level of a kombucha, to be honest."

I've had a shot, and honestly, I wasn't feeling it. "In what, then? Your car parked at the Palazzo's free parking? That's miles away."

He grinned, undeterred. "You make a point there." He pulled out his phone, squinting at the screen. "Uber it is. My treat."

"You don't have to—"

"Relax, Eva. You can pay me back in… let's say, six free cappuccinos. With latte art."

"Six? That's extortion."

"Seven, then. Inflation's a killer."

I rolled my eyes but couldn't help the small smile tugging at my lips. Eric had that effect on me—even when he was being insufferable, he was somehow charming.

"You know," I said, leaning against my car, "most people just ask for a phone number." Screw it all to hell. Tegan's payback was coming in slowly but surely.

Eric feigned innocence. "I'm old-fashioned. I prefer my extortion artisanal. Besides, I'm already in your DMs. Fort Knox settings couldn't keep me away."

I scoffed. "Old-fashioned? You're wearing a pajama suit set."

He looked down, then back at me with a grin. "They're practical. And festive. Like me."

I snorted. "Festive. Right. More like a walking hazard."

He stepped closer, artificial light shining his hair. "Admit it. You'd miss my hazards."

I rolled my eyes, but my smile betrayed me. "I'd miss your Uber account. That's it."

A silver Prius pulled up, its breaks squeaking in protest. Eric stepped forward, suddenly serious. His gaze dropped to my lips, and for a moment, the world seemed to slow down.

"For the record?" he said softly. "This isn't part of the

payment plan."

He leaned in, and my breath hitched. But before he could close the distance, I sidestepped smoothly, yanking the car door open.

"Where's Tegan?" I said, sliding into the Uber.

He scrunched his brow. "Tegan?" He shook his head, a hint of irritation hitting his otherwise cheery face. "Who cares."

I nodded, angry all over again. "Shouldn't you—" but I stopped myself form making a fool of myself. "Cappuccino *numero uno* is on me tomorrow. Don't be late."

Before I closed the door on him, he said, "Missed chance to say, 'don't be a latte!'"

As the car pulled away, I caught a glimpse of Eric standing in the parking lot, his laugh echoing after me.

"I'll bring the hazards!" he shouted.

Fucking Eric.

CHAPTER

EIGHTEEN

SATURDAY MORNING, POST-PILATES, I wafted into the café like a zen goddess who'd just discovered boundary-setting. My mission was to secure my cortado, claim the last raspberry tart (fight me, Karen in Lululemons), and casually pay for Eric's cappuccino with the grace of a woman who's never once wished she could block someone in real life. Tegan's meltdowns were buried deep in my mental junk drawer. Add Scott's sugar daddy role (his wallet's problem) to the file. And Eric's habit of texting emojis at 1 a.m.? Blocked! I was a new Eva—a woman who uses retinol and reads Terms & Conditions. Mostly.

Felicia, however, was thriving in her "hot mess express" era.

"You'll never guess where this souvenir popped up," she hissed, shoving her phone at me. The screen displayed a close-up of what looked like a crime scene photo from *CSI:*

Vampire Diaries.

"Felicia," I gasped. "Is that… a bite mark on your—"

"Inner thigh? Yes. And before you ask—no, it wasn't Nosferatu. Though frankly, a 500-year-old vampire would've had better manners. Think they have higher standards?"

I choked on my cortado. "Why didn't you call me? I could've rescued you!" On my high horse now, but my car hadn't survived the night, what with that flat and all. Phone dead, too—Felicia had been good and well on her own.

"Because you'd have shown up in your pajamas, waving a rolling pin, and I was too busy being a casual queen!" She slumped against the counter, dramatic as a *Romy and Michelle* reunion. "His name is Jason. Or Justin. Or… J-something. He had a tattoo of a dolphin on his—"

"Stop!" I covered my ears. "The mental picture!"

"—ankle. Get your mind out of the gutter, Eva."

We dissolved into giggles, drawing side-eye from a man reading *The Art of War* over a matcha latte.

"Maybe you're allergic to good choices," I said, poking a bruise on her elbow that resembled Australia.

"Or maybe I'm just a girl trying to live," she groaned.

Obvs, Felicia had ghosted her latest Tinder swipe, and

made me swear on my precious gaudy green car not to breathe a word to the girls about her Valentine's Day catastrophe. Lucky the thing had been towed home early this morning, or I'd be stuck swearing on my non-existent love life. I'd keep my promise—though, honestly, resisting the urge to "accidentally" blurt it out during girls' night was as tempting as a Nordstrom Rack sale.

Of course Eric chose to waltz into my life again mid-bite, raspberry tart drippings on my chin. There he was, sliding into the chair opposite me like he hadn't heavily come on to me last night—in a pajama suit set, no less. (A moment my brain had helpfully replayed 4,682 times. Thanks, brain. Really productive.)

"Morning," he said, flashing a happy and clueless grin. His dark blue eyes were doing their usual twinkle-twinkle routine, and his stupid cologne—Eau de Regret?—wafted over like a chemical warfare attack on my common sense.

I forced a smile, channeling the serene energy of a woman sure of herself. "Hi, Eric. Nursing a hangover or are you just here to make me nervous?"

He laughed, scooting closer until our knees nearly touched under the table. Casual. So casual. "Can't it be both?"

I couldn't help a smile. Why was he so sunny? Had he not

just had a screaming match with Tegan the other day? Or was he one of those people who thrived on drama?

"Look, about last night—" he started, raking a hand through his hair in a way that should've been illegal.

"Oh, that?" I cut in, waving a hand like I'd already forgotten the mortifying spectacle of him drunkenly forgetting he had a girlfriend and coming on to me. "Ancient history."

"Right." He cleared his throat. "Still, I'm sorry. I was a total… spaz."

"Spaz?" I arched a brow. "That's the PG version? I'd say you were borderline jackass, perhaps."

He grinned that infuriating, knee-weakening grin. "Fine. I was a jackass."

"A *giant* jackass," I corrected, feeling that flirty light air around us again.

"Guilty." He leaned in, elbows on the table, and my traitorous heart did a backflip. "But in my defense, you wore those jeans that make your—"

"Eric." I held up a hand, channeling my inner high school principal. "If the next words out of your mouth aren't 'I'll never do it again,' I'm defenestrating your coffee."

He chuckled, low and warm, and *oh god*, why did his

laugh have to sound like snuggling a blanket? "Noted. But for the record..." His gaze dropped to my lips for a nanosecond. "I'm not sorry about all of it."

I froze. This was it. The moment my resolve would crumble to bits.

"Apology semi-accepted," I said, standing abruptly and slinging my bag over my shoulder. "But until you Venmo me for emotional damages, you're on probation."

His smile widened. "What's the interest rate?"

"Extortionate," I called over my shoulder, marching fast before my willpower could mutiny.

"Wait!" He called, getting up in a hurry. "What about the cappuccino you owe me?"

I faltered, though, in hindsight, I should've really kept going. "Felicia has it for you. She's got seven IOUs with your name on it."

He just laughed. "Oh come on. Sit with me. I happen to be quite charming when I put an effort."

"It'll take quite the effort," I said, but I was already sitting down, my purse on the empty chair beside me. What can I say? Eric was charming.

Felicia brought his cappuccino order and a second tart, sorry she had to run. Busy Saturday, and all that. I'd said a quick thanks. One down, six to go.

"So," Eric said, flashing that grin that probably worked on everyone except women with self-respect and a working knowledge of toxic exes. "Pilates class, huh? Did you levitate? Achieve inner peace? Discover a new core muscle you never knew existed?"

"Oh, yeah. I orgasmed."

He choked on his cappuccino. "Sorry—*what?*"

"It happens! Not all the time, but sometimes. It's kind of a hit or miss."

He coughed, clearing his throat. "Christ, I see why you like it, then. No wonder you never came for a jiu jitsu lesson."

God, now I was sweating.

"Well..." He leaned forward, elbows on the table, eyes suddenly earnest in a way that made my traitorous pulse skitter. "I'm glad I ran into you today. Because I'd like to revisit some sentiments. Sober this time. Fully caffeinated." He tapped his triple-shot cappuccino. "Dangerously alert."

Oh no. This was veering into rom-com territory. The kind where the heroine forgives the hot mess because he has nice forearms and a puppy-dog smile—and a possible-but-unsure-as-of-yet psychos ex.

"Eva," he said, softer now, and *damn him*, my name sounded like velvet in his mouth. "I've been thinking about you. A lot. And I'd love to take you out. Properly. No tequila, no karaoke, no games, just me. If you'll have me."

For a heartbeat, I nearly folded. That jawline of his—all sharp angles and golden-brown perfection. Those eyes—full of wonder and excitement. But then I remembered. This man had once curved his hands around Tegan's neck. And squeezed.

I had to cut it, and fast. Painfully, too.

"I appreciate the sentiment. And your apology. It was uncomfortable to say the least."

He started. "That's it?"

"Yes."

"There's no pressure on my end, Eva. I just want the chance to go out with you," Eric said, his voice softening. "I'm starting to develop feelings for you, and I'm being completely honest when I say—"

"I'm being honest too, Eric."

"I don't get why you're always so harsh with me," he continued, looking a little defeated. "At first, I thought you were just playing hard to get or maybe nervous, but now I see this is just who you are. You teeter between being nice and an ice queen. I just want to understand. If you tell me why, I'll walk away, I promise."

"Why, what?"

"Why one minute you're telling me about your Pilates coregasms and the next you're dismissing me with a single look. Full disclosure: I like you. I want to see you every day, and if you'll have me, I'd like to do this every day with you. Just sit in this café and talk." He ran a hand through his hair. "I'm actually a nice guy. You'd know that if you give me a chance."

I couldn't help myself. I laughed—more of a scoff, actually. "I cannot believe this," I said, disbelief flooding my voice. My mind immediately flashed to the mess that was Eric and Tegan, and how, no matter how good-looking Eric was, or how charming he was, I did not want to be caught in the middle of it. "And I'd like to know why you're acting like you haven't completely offended me in the worst way possible. The other night at the bar, yesterday on *Valentine's Day*, and again today? Also, news flash, you don't have to announce you're a 'nice guy' if you actually are one."

The cocky gleam in his eyes shifted into confusion, and I found myself wondering how on earth he could act like everything was normal. He couldn't have been too drunk to remember what happened, and there was no way he could blame alcohol for his messy relationship with Tegan.

He was cornered, and he knew it.

"I didn't think it was that bad," Eric said, trying to laugh it off nervously. "Some people might even say I'm charming."

"People like Tegan, I suppose?" I snapped, my voice biting with frustration.

His brow furrowed. "Tegan? What does she have to do with any of this?"

The audacity of him! I couldn't believe it. I'd met plenty of men with low scruples before, but Eric? He was in a league of his own.

I laughed, incredulous. "Please tell me you're joking. You actually thought I'd go along with this? You really thought I was just 'playing hard to get'—is this a joke? Are you honestly going to pretend you have nothing to do with her? Or are you suddenly having second thoughts about the whole open relationship now that Tegan's been officially promoted to sugar baby to some middle-aged trust fund guy after a scandalous first date involving erotic asphyxiation? Or do I have to remind you how you unscrupulously came on to me while you were in a committed relationship with Tegan?"

"A committed relationship with Tegan?" Eric's voice was sharp enough to cut glass. "Where the hell do you get that idea?"

"From the source herself! Tegan told me the first day I ran into her out in the snow that you two were a couple. I knew everything before I met you, Eric. Lexi even told me all about Tegan and her sugar baby contract with Scott. You know about Scott, right? You have to know. I'm sure you know all about it, I don't have to fill you in. You're probably encouraging her to marry him for his money with your open relationship or whatever you two have going on.

"I'll tell you one thing, though—I will never take Tegan's sloppy seconds, and baby, you're sloppy. The sloppiest there is. I want nothing to do with either of you. In fact, you disgust me." I sat back on my chair, proud of myself for finally speaking up and spilling all I'd had bubbled up in me.

He was speechless, which only made me feel better because it confirmed what I already knew.

I won.

When he finally spoke, he said, "So, that's how low you think of me. No wonder you were always so cold towards me."

"How else did you expect me to be? Welcoming? Charmed? Did you want me to feel special that you chose me as a second to Tegan? Oh, look. A UFC fighter wants me as a sneaky link. How special."

"No. I suppose not," he said, almost a whisper.

"Eva, stop!" Felicia said, running to my side. She shook her head, but I wasn't interested in what she had to say. Not now. I was too mad, and too wound up. I looked at Eric again, feeling on top of the world for finally using my voice.

The look of confusion on his face dropped my steel-strong confidence just a tad.

Felicia said, "Oh god. I should've told you sooner."

"Told me what?" I asked, more confused than ever. My heart sank to my knees. I looked at Felicia for support, but she only looked shocked.

"We were wrong, Eva. We were wrong about everything. Tegan has done nothing but lie."

I wasn't understanding anything. Slowly, I looked at Eric.

"Tegan has never been, nor will she ever be my girlfriend," he said, and my vision tunneled.

"What?" I almost whispered, feeling myself go weak. I was fainting, surely.

"Yoooo!" A guy in a tracksuit lunged from behind a potted fern, phone locked in. "This shit is crazy! UFC's Eric

Mann mid meltdown—live on my Insta! Smash that share button, fam!"

Felicia and I looked at the man with the phone, and Eric muttered something under his breath. The man recording held his phone up, filming the whole thing going from Eric to me to Felicia.

"Hey!" Felicia said, and lunged at him. "You can't film here!"

I closed my eyes, wishing the earth would swallow me up.

"Fucking Tegan."

Please turn the page for a sneak peek

into Girl Fight Series book 2

SPRING BLUES

available now.

SPRING BLUES

Girl Fight Book 2

CHAPTER

ONE

SPRING HIT THE VALLEY like a midlife crisis—sudden, sweaty, and relentless. By noon, the heat had already sent three tourists to the ER with quick onset dehydration, the heat so intense they reportedly tried to drink the Venetian gondola water. *Eww.*

It came like a tornado, but instead of wind, heat.

That's Vegas, baby.

All neon glitter and bottomless mimosas until you remember it's built on a desert that's basically Satan's personal sauna. (Or, if you're Felicia-level crude, Satan's asshole.)

Survival tip 101: SPF 100 and a therapist on speed dial.

And a hydration pack?

I slumped in my car—a gaudy green thing with the personality of a depressed tortoise—debating whether to suffocate in stale AC or roast like a rotisserie chicken. The fresh air option was a joke. Opening the window felt like sticking my face in a hair dryer set to vengeance.

My phone buzzed, Felicia texting she was "omw!!"

(Translation: "I haven't left the café yet and I've just remembered I have to bake a batch of muffins. Sorry!")

I groaned. Felicia's "omw" was less a promise and more a threat. Last week, "omw" meant she was meant to leave on time, but you see, Shane didn't know how to operate the La Marzocco and she had to teach him, and could I be a dear and wait an hour? Maybe two. Today? I'd be lucky if she arrived before the asphalt melted.

The heat shimmered off the parking lot, warping the

Strip's skyline into a Dali painting. I missed winter. Those crisp mornings when my breath fogged the air and my bad decisions felt... cooler. *Next year*, I vowed, *I'll appreciate snowflakes instead of grumping through them like disgruntled sour grapes.*

Lies. All lies.

Spring had arrived with its heat and color, and my life was stuck in B&W. It wasn't just bleak. Bleak was too kind. Bleak implied a moody Scandinavian film with artistic lighting. Mine was more low-budget rom-com directed by a sleep-deprived intern starring Eva Torres, star of the viral video One Night In *Hell*!

Embarrassing? Let's just say if shame were a currency, I could've bought the Bellagio. Twice.

I flicked the AC knob. It coughed out air that smelled suspiciously of regret and Dollar Tree sunscreen. Outside, a tour group shuffled past, their sun hats drooping like wilted lettuce. One woman fanned herself with a poker chip.

Felicia's ETA pinged in my head: 7-10 business days.

To pass the time, I counted the cracks in my dashboard. (Twelve. One resembled Harry Styles.)

The steering wheel burned my palms. I sighed. At this rate, my car would double as a sweat lodge. Maybe I could monetize it? Vegas's newest attraction: The Sauna of Shame!

Last week, waiting for Felicia had been almost pleasant. I'd parked a block and a half away from Desert Bloom by the florist's shop, where bougainvillea spilled over the wall like a Pinterest dream. The owner—a woman who looked like she'd been born holding a pair of pruning shears—had side-eyed my car at first. But once she realized I wasn't casing the joint, just loitering for 20 minutes max, she'd warmed up. She even waved once, which I took as permission to keep freeloading on her floral ambiance.

Note to self: Buy a bouquet. Or at least a single carnation.

Today, though? The bougainvillea looked as wilted as my will to live. I cracked the window, hoping for a whiff of floral serenity, but all I got was a face full of Sahara-grade heat.

Nine minutes down. One to ten to go.

Just as I was about to reset my mental timer, I spotted her. She was power-walking like a woman on a mission, clutching two iced drinks like they were the Holy Grail. Her curls bounced with every step, and her apron—a masterpiece of flour smudges and coffee stains—dangled precariously off one shoulder.

"You're alive!" I called as she yanked open the passenger

door.

"Barely," she panted, thrusting a drink at me. "I think I just sweated out my soul."

I started the car and the AC kicked in full-force, filling the space with the scent of iced cortado and stale milk.

"Sorry for making you walk," I said, not entirely sorry. The alternative—showing my face at the café—was unthinkable. And with good reason, too.

Felicia flopped into the seat, fanning herself with a napkin. "So. Eric was at the café today."

My stomach did a backflip. "Today?"

She raised an eyebrow, clearly too dehydrated to mock me for my overeager tone.

"First time I've seen him in weeks," she added, sipping her drink like it held the secrets of the universe.

"Oh, really," I said, aiming for casual and landing somewhere between "awkward" and "full-on panic."

Felicia smirked. "Yep. He asked about you."

Let me set the scene: Eric Mann—UFC fighter, possessor of a jawline so sharp it could probably file taxes— was a staple at the café. And by "staple," I mean every Saturday at 9 a.m., he'd go in, order a cappuccino, and flash a grin that turned my bones to marshmallow. It was hardly my fault.

This, of course, was before my ex–best friend, Tegan—a human Insta post—declared him her "soulmate" via an elaborate web of lies that would've made *Pretty Little Liars* blush. Spoiler: They weren't soulmates. They weren't even *soupmates*.

The last time I saw Eric, I'd channeled Shakespearean levels of drama in a café full of gawking strangers, while a UFC fanatic live-streamed my meltdown. The video, titled "Caffeine & Chaos: Love Triangle KO!" now has 3 million views and a comment section arguing whether I'm a "girlboss" or "needs therapy." (*Por que no los dos?*)

Weeks later, the theories persist. Am I Eric's secret wife? A scorned Tinder swipe? A CIA agent investigating latte fraud? The truth? Buried deeper than my gym membership card.

"You should come back," Felicia announced, sidling up to me with the sly grin—or the start of a heat stroke. "Reclaim your Saturdays! Pilates, cortados, that little moan you make when the espresso hits…" She paused, dangling the bait. "Maybe I can save you the last raspberry tart. I'll hide it in my underboob. It'll be squished, but you'll get it, promise!"

I groaned. "You're evil." Ever since the viral video, the café'd been swimming in patrons—which meant, "Sorry Eva, the tarts are sold out!"

Felicia rolled her eyes. "Babe, the internet's moved on. They're all obsessed with a squirrel that learned to skateboard."

"But what if Eric's there? What if he—"

"So what!" She nudged me. "Come on. Your cortisol levels need that tart more than I need a weekend in Hawaii."

"I could use a weekend in Hawaii!" Truth was, I missed it. My Saturdays were more than a routine—they were my foundation. Pilates for the body, caffeine for the soul, and people-watching so prime I'd started mentally casting strangers in rom-coms. (That elderly man with the dachshund? Clearly a retired spy.)

I missed it. More than missed it. Craved it like I craved sunlight and cool air and margaritas and laughter. The misunderstanding of the decade had thrown me into a little depression of sorts, even if it was hard to admit. And a little promise of raspberry tart wasn't good enough to drag me out of it.

"Honestly? I think he's over it."

I glanced at Felicia, stopped at a red light. Her eyes were

doing that thing where they looked like they'd been Photoshopped too big, and her hands were jittering so much her iced cortado was practically doing a tap dance. Was it the caffeine? The sun? Or just her desperate attempt to avoid another too-sunny walk tomorrow?

Or—and this was the kicker—maybe she genuinely thought I should just bite it and move on. Who didn't make viral mistakes once in a while?

And I would've moved on, too, if the universe hadn't decided to remind me every time I opened my phone. "UFC Fuckboy & Café Meltdown Girl Strikes!" the headlines screamed. (Okay, fine, it was just Instagram, but still.)

"I called him a disgusting pig," I groaned, gripping the steering wheel like it might teleport me to a parallel universe. "He's not over that. *I'm* not over that."

Felicia tilted her head, squinting like she was trying to recall the exact wording. "I think you just said he disgusts you. Not the pig part."

I blinked. "That's any better?"

"Marginally."

I buried my face in my hands, the embarrassment hitting me like a rogue wave. "It couldn't have been worse."

"It could've," she said, her tone a perfect blend of

sympathy and "can we please talk about something else now?"

"Trust me, Fel. He's not over it. The internet's not over it. Even my dry cleaner brought it up last week."

I pulled into my parking spot, the shade doing absolutely nothing to combat the heat. But I wasn't done yet. I flung open the door, braving the sauna-like air to keep the conversation alive.

"Yeah," Felicia said, though I wasn't entirely sure what she was agreeing to. "But today he asked how you were. I think he gets it was all a misunderstanding. He's not going to hold it against you forever."

My heart did this weird thing where it stopped, then started again like it was on a defibrillator. "He really asked about me?"

A rush of blood flooded my cheeks—part embarrassment, part something else I couldn't quite name. Maybe Felicia was right. Maybe enough time had passed. Maybe we could be friendly again. And maybe, I'd feel brave enough to pick her up at the café instead of lurking by the florist like a creepy stalker.

Felicia flashed a grin, her iced coffee sweating almost as much as we were. "He did. I told him you're still mortified— but thawing, just taking your sweet time. And please thaw,

Eva. My blisters have blisters from walking to the damn florist. It's a block and a half! And with this heat, too." She wiggled her foot for dramatic effect.

My gut still knotted at the thought, but a tiny, reckless voice chirped, *If Eric can slide into the café like he's on* Love Island, *why can't you?* Then again, Eric's idea of "confrontation" involved octagons and spandex. Mine involved hiding behind potted ferns.

"I'll Venmo you an Uber," I bargained, fanning myself with too-warm air. "I'm just not ready to be Café Meltdown Girl: The Sequel."

"Girl, bye," Felicia snapped, her patience evaporating faster than her cortado condensation. "This isn't about the ride. Why can't you get that?"

"But—"

"I'm not finished," she interrupted, her voice rising like a kettle about to whistle. "I'm at the café every day. Eric's back. Even the guy who tried to pay with Monopoly money is back. Why can't you stop hiding?"

I slumped deeper into the driver's seat, now approximately the temperature of a baked Alaska. "I'm not hiding. I'm strategically avoiding."

"Call it what you want." She flopped back, her curls

sticking to the headrest. "But someday you'll wake up, 90 years old, yelling at cats about a TikTok literally no one else remembers. Live, Eva. Or Tegan wins."

"Tegan's a sociopath. She'd wear a scandal like it's Zara's new collection."

"Be like me, then!" Felicia gestured wildly, nearly elbowing her door. "I'm out here, unbothered, going to the café day in, day out. People recognize me, but *so what*? It's literally not that hard."

"Fine," I huffed, defeated. "Tomorrow'll be a café pickup, no more block and a half walk to the florist. But if someone mentions the video, I'm blaming you."

"Deal." She smirked, tapping her phone. "Besides, Eric's still trending on Twitter—I mean, X. Silver linings, yeah?"

I gaped. "His career's one meme away from collapse."

"*Pfft*. UFC's all about drama. He's probably thriving." She flung open the car door, desert heat rushing in like an uninvited in-law. "Now, can we please get out of this mobile sauna before I melt into a puddle of iced coffee?"

AUTHOR'S NOTE

Hi, reader! Thank you for reading my story. I loved getting to know Eva and friends and I hope you loved them too.

If you feel up to it, please sign up to my newsletter! I'm not a spammer, so if you get an email every once in a while when I'm updating on new releases or bonus chapters, then it's something!

Subsribe to Blair's Newsletter

As an indie author, reviews are our lifeline. Please leave a review (if you want to!) on Amazon, Goodreads, or The StoryGraph.

Thank you for supporting me! It means the world.

P.S. Drop a line if you want to be in my ARC Team! Email at: authorblairmonroy@gmail.com.

About the Author

Blair Monroy writes funny rom-coms with memorable characters who love hard and play hard. When not writing, she's hanging out by the pool with rosé in one hand and a book in the other.

Girl Fight is the first book in the Girl Fight series.

IG: @blairmonroyauthor

TikTok: @authorblairmonroy

Email: authorblairmonroy@gmail.com

Books by Blair Monroy

GIRL FIGHT SERIES

Girl Fight

Spring Blues

Summer Storm

Autumn Falling